A Chill in the Lane

A CHILL IN THE LANE

by
Mabel Esther Allan

THOMAS NELSON INC.
NASHVILLE / NEW YORK

Copyright © 1974 by Mabel Esther Allan

All rights reserved under International and Pan-American Conventions. Published in Nashville, Tennessee, by Thomas Nelson Inc., and distributed in Canada by Thomas Nelson & Sons (Canada) Limited. Manufactured in the United States of America.

First edition

Library of Congress Cataloging in Publication Data

Allan, Mabel Esther.
    A chill in the lane.

    SUMMARY: While vacationing in Cornwall with her family, a sixteen-year-old adopted girl finds herself strangely and frighteningly involved with the past.
    [1. Supernatural—Fiction]   I. Title.
PZ7.A4Ch   [Fic]   74–733
ISBN 0–8407–6384–0

Alsach +

Contents

A Chill in the Lane

CHAPTER ONE

Trelonyan Cove

Sitting in the back of the shabby old car with her brothers on either side of her, Lyd Allbright suddenly wanted to scream. Tom, who was fifteen, and Jeff, one year younger, were well-grown boys, and she was cramped between them. To add to her discomfort, Collie, the family dog, was sitting on her feet and making them hotter than ever.

Their luggage was in the trunk, with cans of food and packs of cornflakes, but in the back seat with them were many other things: a box containing sheets and pillow-cases, the boys' and her father's rods and fishing lines, two baskets for the fish they hoped to catch, Collie's old blanket . . . all kinds of odds and ends.

The car smelled strongly of dog and, slightly, of overheated human bodies. The front windows were open, but the back windows had been stuck for a long time. It was a very old car, and their father had said he didn't think it would last much longer. After that they'd have to do without, because he couldn't afford to buy another one.

Lyd writhed a little, moving her hot, bare arm away from contact with Tom's. At sixteen she *couldn't* scream.

She was almost grown up, far too old to give way to her old fears and moods. She had learned to control them, to keep them secret, but that didn't mean they weren't there. And one thing she still feared and hated was to be in a cramped, hot space and unable to get out.

I ought to have said I wouldn't go, she told herself. She did try, but Dad and Mother had seemed so hurt.

The chance of a cottage in Cornwall for two weeks had seemed like a wonderful bonus to the other four. They couldn't believe it when Mr. Allbright came home from work and announced that one of the men at the factory—his foreman—couldn't go because of sickness in his family, and that the rent was already paid. *Someone* might as well enjoy it, the foreman had said. Fred Allbright had three kids, so for a nominal payment the cottage had become his.

Lyd very much wanted to see Cornwall, but she had known from the beginning that she was going to hate the long car trip. She had suggested that she go youth hosteling with a school friend instead, but her father had dismissed the idea at once.

"You're too young," he said. "I don't approve of girls of your age wandering off on their own. Maybe next year."

"And we want you with us, Lyd." Her mother's voice had sounded hurt. "It will be a wonderful vacation. We couldn't enjoy it without you."

Lyd looked ahead at her parents' backs. Her father was a fair, tired-looking man, who always seemed worried, and her mother was fair too, with a pale, pretty face. Tom and Jeff were very much like them.

They had left Bristol early in the morning, but the August traffic had been heavy, especially around Exeter, and they had not yet crossed the River Tamar.

"When do we get to Cornwall?" Lyd asked, trying not to sound as desperate as she felt.

"I think we should reach the bridge soon," her father answered. "We'll stop and have our picnic when we find a quiet place on the other side. It's getting late; I know you must all be hungry."

"Are you very uncomfortable, Lyd?" her mother asked, turning around to glance at the three in the back.

"She's wriggling around like a snake," said Tom amiably. He and Jeff had passed the time by talking about football teams and commenting on some of the cars they passed.

"There isn't room to wriggle much," Lyd said. "I have an insect bite on my ankle, and another way up my leg. I can't even scratch."

"It's a long way yet," said Mr. Allbright. He wasn't too sure of the car and would be thankful when they reached the cottage, which was only a few miles from the western end of Cornwall.

Suddenly they came to the long bridge. The wide River Tamar gleamed below them, and a salty breeze quickly improved the air in the back of the car. For a short while Lyd forgot her discomfort, her suppressed fear. They were heading toward the very end of England. Cornwall was a county so cut off that it was almost a foreign land. At one time the people there had even spoken a different language.

"I'm Cornish," she said, as they reached Saltash. "I was born here, wasn't I?"

There were a few moments of silence. Then her father said, "Your birth was registered in Bodmin."

His voice was stiff, and Lyd felt hot again. She knew she shouldn't have mentioned the subject, but she couldn't stop. It was as if her tongue had a life of its own.

"So maybe I had a romantic Cornish name."

"You didn't," Mr. Allbright said flatly, in the calm, no-nonsense tone he had nearly always used when Lyd tried to talk about her beginnings. "You were called Pratt or Platt. I forget which."

"Don't you even *remember?*"

"Why should he?" Jeff interrupted. "You've been Lyd Allbright since you were about four. You're just one of the family, so stop being an idiot."

It was good, really, to be one of the family, and most of the time Lyd didn't want to remember that she had had a different start. It couldn't matter; almost always she had been convinced that she was loved as much as, or more than, the boys. Yet lately she had been thinking about it more than usual, and when anyone was annoyed with her she had those awful niggling little doubts.

Sometimes over the years she had asked herself: I won-er if they've ever wanted to get rid of me, if they've ever been sorry they adopted me.

The natural follow-up to that had been to wonder what her real parents had been like. All she knew was that they had died in an accident when she was two.

Lyd had imagination and the boys had not. Sometimes her mother said, "Stop romancing, Lyd. Oh, I know it may be useful to you one day. Maybe you'll write books or something. But you have to live life as it is."

The trouble was that life was often so difficult, and a dream world could be so comforting. But now she was sixteen—almost old enough to be married—and she ought to be able to get a grip on things.

She glanced at Tom and then at Jeff. They were so big and placid; they never seemed really troubled by anything. They were not clever, but they were kind and warmhearted, and Lyd knew very well that they were both devoted to her. She was the eldest, but she was small for her age and very dark, with dark-brown hair, dark eyes, and high cheekbones.

"Is this your sister?" people had sometimes asked in surprise. "She isn't at all like you."

Lyd had a secret desire to be like them. She admired their looks and thought herself rather plain. It was awful to be an adopted daughter, especially when your parents were rather poor. One of her most pressing worries was that she wondered if she ought to leave school and start earning her living. Why should they keep on supporting her?

They ate their picnic lunch in a country lane with high banks on either side. Collie was given a bone and some hard pieces of toast, and after he had crunched everything up he looked around for rabbits, but found none. Lyd walked up and down for a few minutes, breathing deeply, but soon it was time to go back to the car and continue the journey.

On and on they went, through the long miles of Cornwall, and then at last they were approaching the town of Penzance. The sight of blue Mount's Bay, with the island called St. Michael's Mount rising from the water, revived them all. Before long they had left even Penzance behind, and also the fishing port of Newlyn, and were climbing a steep hill into the rather bleak, bare country of the Land's End Peninsula. It was country that struck Lyd to the heart in a strange way. But oh! she couldn't bear the confines of the car much longer.

They came at last to a signpost half buried in leaves. "Trelonyan Cove, 1½ miles," it said, pointing down a narrow lane.

"Trelonyan is a beautiful name," said Mrs. Allbright. She, too, longed to arrive at their destination, because she had a bad headache and wanted a cup of tea.

"It seems I've heard that name before," said her husband. "I said so the day Bill Johnson told me about the cottage. But I've never been to West Cornwall."

As he cautiously turned the car onto the narrow lane, the high banks on either side almost touched the paint-work on the fenders. Foxgloves, red campion, trails of honeysuckle, and a variety of ferns grew along the way. The sea was nearby, but you would not have thought so. Mr. Allbright mused about fishing from a boat on calm blue water, then, at the sound of an argument, said sharply over his shoulder:

"Stop that, you lot! In ten minutes or less you can stretch your legs." Then he had to brake and back into a slightly wider part of the road to allow two cars to crawl past. They were filled with people flushed with the sun, and one car had a boat fastened on top.

"Tom is leaning on me. I can't bear it!" Lyd complained. Since they had stopped for the picnic she had been sitting on the outside, with Tom in the middle, but it hadn't helped much.

"I am not. Your great sharp elbow is sticking in my ribs," said Tom.

"And Collie won't sit on anyone else's feet. He's always on mine."

"He's only a third your dog," Jeff remarked, "but he loves you best."

"The sooner we get there the better," said Mrs. All-bright. Then she whispered to her husband, "Lyd hasn't got over it. I really hoped she had. She gets claustrophobia or something in the car, and it *is* uncomfortable back there. I should have let her sit in the front, but I'm bigger than she is."

"Well, we really won't be long now."

The car had started again, but soon had to come to another halt, as two more cars came up from the Cove.

Lyd peered out at the feathery, flowery banks. The deep, tree-arched lane was in shadow, but the car felt no cooler. It would be wonderful to be *there,* to swim, perhaps, before dark. And, once there, maybe she wouldn't be a prey to fears anymore. She would just have a glorious vacation by the sea.

They were going down the lane slowly and carefully. Once again Tom's arm stuck to Lyd's thin one. She moved fractionally and tried to think of the Cove they would soon see. The high banks were suddenly lower, though the lane was as narrow and winding as ever. Lyd peered into the green, cool-looking wood on the left. There must be a stream, for she caught the sudden glint of water.

Then it happened. Lyd went rigid and her whole body was washed with sudden cold. For a moment everything went blank, almost black.

Tom was instantly aware of it.

"Lyd's going to faint!" he cried warningly. "She's gone green. What's up, Lyd? Do you feel sick?"

"Oh, try and hold on for just a few minutes more, dear," said Mrs. Allbright, turning around.

Lyd gulped and found that she could see and speak again. "I'm not sick. It was just cold."

"Cold?" They all echoed her words incredulously. "It's like an oven."

"The wood . . . the lane . . . something," Lyd murmured, still dazed. "This is a bad place!"

"That's enough of that!" her father said irritably. "Don't let's have any of your romantic nonsense now, Lyd. You were sixteen three months ago. You ought to have more sense."

Lyd was silent. She felt humiliated as well as upset. He was only saying what she had often thought herself, but it certainly hadn't been romantic nonsense this time. What she had felt had been involuntary and real.

They drove slowly down a steep hill and took a final bend. Trelonyan Cove was still hidden by trees and high banks where the blackberries grew big and red, but now they could see great cliffs on either side and the vivid dark-blue of the sea.

"We're here!" cried Mrs. Allbright. "There's nothing bad, Lyd. You're just too hot and cramped. It's a beautiful lane. You'll be walking along it dozens of times."

Lyd shuddered and Collie whined, shifting off her feet.

In a hollow by a stream stood a tiny combined store and post office, closed, because it was after five-thirty. There was also an inn called the Trelonyan Arms, built of Cornish granite and very small. It had tables outside, and a few tourists were sitting at them, drinking beer or lemonade and eating potato chips. Mr. Allbright got out of the car and went to ask for directions.

"The cottage is up that side lane there," he explained, when he returned. "Only a minute, the innkeeper said."

As he turned the car toward the lane they all saw a little board that showed the words "Tamarisk Cottage" in faded white letters. The lane climbed and was very rough, but suddenly they found themselves on a stretch of grass behind the cottage. The house was whitewashed, and on two sides of it tamarisk hedges waved in the breeze.

In wild excitement they all struggled to get out of the

car. Lyd stretched her bare legs sideways and wriggled free. Then she was standing upright in the beautiful hot air, which smelled of the sea and flowers and grass. She bent to scratch her ankle, then leaned back into the car.

"Where's my red shoulder bag?"

"Here!" Jeff tossed it to her. "With all your worldly wealth in it."

"No," said Lyd, gay now that she was free. "I still have three pounds in the Savings Bank."

"It's her diary she's worrying about," teased Tom, evading Collie, who, with wildly waving tail, was dancing around them. "She puts all her secret thoughts into that diary."

"If you ever read it, Tom Allbright, I'll never forgive you," threatened Lyd.

Tom grinned. "Me? I'm not interested in girlish dreams."

"No. He's only interested in football," said Jeff. "Let's go and look around before we unpack the car."

Lyd ran eagerly around the cottage. In front was a tiny garden, where roses and delphiniums grew, and below was the Cove, held in the arms of the two cliffs. There was a stone quay curving around blue water, for the tide was high. The sides of the cliffs were grim and stony, and in the hollow where the stream ran out into the harbor were several old stone lofts and warehouses, all derelict, and about half a dozen stone cottages. There was no smoke rising from their chimneys.

Lyd leaned on the prickly grass and stones of the bank and gazed downward. The sun beat on her thin blouse and warmed her body. She took several deep breaths, feeling alive and comfortable again.

Behind her the others were talking. A strange voice was among them . . . a deep, burring voice with a lilt in it.

"I'm Mrs. Pendennis from the post office. I knew you had the extra key, but I'm the one who keeps an eye on the place for the owners. You must be exhausted, my dears. Such a long drive, and isn't it hot? There's an electric kettle in the cottage. It won't take a minute to boil."

"Oh, how wonderful!" cried Mrs. Allbright. "All I want is a cup of tea."

"And I brought you a few things. Bread, eggs, and milk, and a nice bit of boiled ham. There's lettuce in the garden. You'll find the vegetable patch just around the other side. It's gone to seed a little, but it'll be eatable. You can pay me later. I'll leave you all to settle in. Goodbye, my dears." She said "my dears" in a warm, friendly way.

Collie was rolling on the ground, his feathery tail beating up soil and dust. The boys had gone to unload the car, but Lyd followed her mother into the cottage, which was cool and smelled faintly musty, with a fascinating cottage-y aroma. There was a simple living room with old, plain furniture, and a small kitchen with a stone floor.

Upstairs there were three very small bedrooms, reached by a dark staircase built into the wall. Lyd wandered from one room to another, then she leaned over the stairs and called, "Mother! Come and look! Can I have the room at the back?"

Mrs. Allbright reluctantly gave up preparations for a quick meal and toiled up the stairs. The window of the back room gave a view of the car and of the grassy, rocky space. Lyd was glancing at herself in the small mirror. In her red blouse and gray shorts she looked very small and young, but she was putting on lipstick.

"I wish I weren't so plain," she said.

"Plain! You're not plain," said her mother. "When you get more flesh on your bones, you'll be a really pretty girl."

"But I wish I were fair like you."

Mrs. Allbright was silent. Once, when Lyd was five years old, she had called her "my changeling daughter" in a rare burst of imagination. She had always been rather guiltily conscious that she loved this adopted child more than her own boys, but had never felt it wise to tell Lyd so. In any case, she found it difficult to talk about her deepest feelings.

"Mother, can I have this room?"

"But wouldn't you like a view over the Cove, love? The boys won't mind. They'll have to share a bed in either case."

"No, thanks. I'd like this one." Lyd sounded brusque and unfriendly, and knew it.

"Do stop scratching those insect bites. I'll find you something soothing to put on them when I've unpacked. Why don't you want a view of Trelonyan Cove, Lyd?"

"I don't, that's all." Lyd hesitated. If she explained her feelings it would sound like more "romantic nonsense." "It's strange," she said, "but I don't think anyone lives in those houses. It isn't pretty."

Mrs. Allbright glanced at Lyd's set little face under the untidy dark-brown hair. Then she walked into one of the bedrooms that overlooked the Cove. Lyd was right; it wasn't pretty. Even under such a dark-blue sky and with such wonderful blue water, it had a grim air, as if life had gone from it. Yet there were a few boats drawn up on the stones at the beginning of the quay and even a car or two still parked dangerously on the narrow stone stretch that ended with what might once have been an iron beacon.

"I suppose you can have whichever room you like," she said over her shoulder. "But I hope you aren't going to be silly. What *happened* in the lane?"

Lyd had followed her, running a comb through her hair.

"I don't know, Mother. It was the lane and the wood. The feeling went away very quickly. It was just *there,* where I could see the stream."

Mrs. Allbright made a clucking sound and clattered down the stairs. Her attractive face was often anxiously creased, and now it was more troubled than usual. She had a really bad headache, but a cup of tea might cure that.

Lyd stood hesitating. She shouldn't have said anything. Usually the habit of secrecy, established in self-defense as she grew older, would have held. But she had been really disturbed by her reactions in the lane.

After a few moments she followed her mother down the stairs.

CHAPTER TWO

Saul

The boys and Mr. Allbright were coming in and out, carrying suitcases and boxes. Lyd went to help her mother with tea, and soon they were all sitting around the old wooden table in the living room, eating the ham with lettuce hastily gathered and washed. The bread was crusty and fresh, the butter was delicious.

By the time they had finished, it was nearly seven o'clock.

"Now there's a lot to do," said Mrs. Allbright.

At once there was an indignant outcry from Tom and Jeff. "We want to go down and see the Cove first before it gets dark. Couldn't we swim? It's so hot!"

The two adults looked at each other.

"No swimming tonight," Mr. Allbright said. "We have to find a safe place. I heard something about a sandy beach, but I don't see it. I know you all swim well, but you must be careful, especially at first."

"Well, just to take a look, Dad!" Jeff pleaded. "We'll be back in thirty minutes."

21

"All right, go on. I'll help your mother wash the dishes, but after this, it's to be turn about with all the jobs, and no shirking. We want to enjoy ourselves the same as you."

Tom rose, pushing back his chair. He was as tall as his father and was handsome and strong.

"Coming with us, Lyd?" he asked.

Lyd hesitated. She did want to be near the water and to see if anyone lived in those cottages near the Cove.

"All right."

Accompanied by Collie, they ran down the lane they had driven up earlier. Insects hummed in the undergrowth, and Lyd stopped to pick a huge foxglove covered with heavy bells. There were still one or two people outside the Trelonyan Arms, but otherwise the whole place was quiet.

Another hundred yards of narrow, tree-arched road brought them to the stretch of land by the harbor. Fuchsias hung down over an old wall and the water was so blue it dazzled their eyes.

"We can fish off the end of the quay," said Jeff.

"Yes. But sometimes we'll rent a boat and try proper sea fishing. That chap at Dad's factory said you could rent them here."

"Newlyn Harbor was crammed with fishing boats," Jeff remarked. "I wonder why there are none here. Maybe they're out at sea."

"I don't believe they are," said Lyd. "I don't think there are any at all. I read a book about Cornwall. I took it out of the library when I knew we were coming here."

The two boys looked at her indulgently. Lyd was clever. She liked reading and was doing very well at school. It seemed possible that she would stay on until she was old enough to go to a university. They both thought reading was a waste of time, unless it was a help in learning practical things, like how to fish better—details about flies and rods, for instance.

"And . . ." prompted Tom.

"Well, there was a chapter about the fishing industry. It said that some of the smaller harbors are unused nowadays, except by pleasure craft. I suppose this is one of them."

"Did it actually mention Trelonyan Cove?"

"No, it didn't. I looked in the index. And there wasn't time to get another book. We only knew last week that we were coming here. But I think . . ." She frowned at the scene before them.

"You mean you think no one lives here? No fishermen? The cottages do look empty."

They crossed the stream by a stone bridge and saw that the cottages were indeed uninhabited, and in some cases almost derelict. The shadow cast by the western cliff was beginning to touch them. They looked sad and terribly abandoned. But behind a deserted stone building that might once have held fishing gear sat another cottage. Smoke rose in a thin curl from the chimney.

"Look! There's a boy!" cried Lyd. "A young man . . . sitting on that bank."

"So there is," agreed Tom. "Let's go and speak to him."

The boy had seen them and he jumped off the bank and walked toward them. He looked around seventeen, and he wore old trousers and an open-necked white shirt. Tom, looking at his dark hair, dark eyes, and high cheekbones, suddenly thought that he looked like Lyd. Maybe there was something in that talk about Lyd being Cornish.

"Hello!" the stranger said when he was near enough.

"Do you live here?" asked Tom.

"Yes." He nodded at the cottage with the curling smoke.

"Good! As a native you'll be able to tell us things. We've just arrived."

The boy looked at Tom and Jeff gravely, but in a friendly way. Then he glanced at Lyd and smiled.

"I'm a native now, you might say. I've lived here for more than a year." His voice had the same tone as Mrs. Pendennis', and Lyd found herself loving the deep lilt of it. "Before that we lived in Newlyn. My dad was a fisherman. Then he had an accident and retired. You must be the Allbrights."

"How did you know?" asked Jeff.

"Oh, Mrs. Pendennis mentioned you, and so did Mrs. Clark at the inn. There are so few of us here that strangers are interesting, you know. I'm Saul Treporth."

"I'm Tom and this is Jeff. And this is our sister, Lyd."

"Lid? Lid of the teapot or the kettle?" Saul smiled as he said it, as if well aware that he was making a feeble joke.

Lyd was on her dignity at once. "That's an old joke," she said severely. "I'm Lydia, but everyone uses that funny short name. I'm sixteen."

"I beat you then," said Saul, "for I was seventeen last November."

The boys were growing impatient. They had promised to be back in thirty minutes, and there would be trouble if they weren't. Their father was usually a mild man, but he expected to be obeyed.

"We want to know about renting boats, and where it's safe to swim," Tom said.

"Oh, my father owns all the boats," Saul explained easily. "He can let you have any fishing gear you need. That's what he does now. It's seasonal, of course, but he had to do something. He's only forty-two and more or less a cripple. He slipped on a frozen deck." No one would have detected from Saul's tone the months of agony and heartbreak that had followed his father's accident, or of the bitternesss he felt over the dangers of the life of a fisherman. "You can swim from a sandy beach if you just scramble over the point there." He waved his hand in a westward direction. "It's safe enough there. *I* swim in the harbor."

Tom was a trifle nettled. This young man, only two years older than he, seemed to him far too assured and amused.

"We will too, I suppose. Maybe not Lyd, although she swims fairly well. It looks like a good place. Let's walk to the end of the quay, Jeff, before we go back to the cottage."

Lyd stayed behind, close to a glowing fuchsia hedge where the shadows didn't fall. The purple-red flowers were vivid in the late sunlight. Even her insect bites had ceased to bother her now, and the cold terror of the lane was forgotten for the moment. Saul Treporth attracted her strongly.

"You aren't like your brothers," said Saul.

"Don't you think so?" Lyd hedged.

"Not a bit like. They're so big and fair, and you're so little and dark. You look Cornish, or perhaps Welsh—Celtic, anyway."

Lyd was startled. "I *am* Cornish. That is, I think I was born in Cornwall. But in East Cornwall, I believe. My birth was registered in Bodmin."

"How?" Saul was looking puzzled. "I thought you all came from Bristol. Allbright isn't a Cornish name."

"Nor was my real name. Pratt or Platt. I wish I knew which, but Dad doesn't remember. But I really was born in Cornwall."

"Your *father* doesn't remember?"

Lyd was standing with her back to the brilliant glare of the evening sun. She clasped her hands behind her.

"I'm adopted, you see."

"Oh!" He looked taken aback, almost embarrassed.

"I don't mind. I've always known. They love me just as much."

"I'm sure they do," Saul said quickly. "They must have *chosen* you."

Lyd grinned. It made her look quite different. "How tactful of you. That's what people always say to adopted children, you know. That's the kind of advice that's always given in magazines and places. I knew that when I was around ten."

Saul looked increasingly more alert, as though aware he was faced with a sharp intelligence. "I'm sorry," he said contritely. "I didn't mean to be obvious. How did it happen? Do you mind talking about it?"

"Sometimes. My parents, my adoptive parents, don't like it if I do. I *was* chosen, in a kind of way, but only to be a foster child at first. I don't know much about it, except that my real parents were killed in an accident when I was two. There was no one to take me, so I went to an orphanage . . . a children's home. And Mother—my mother now—was wishing for a girl. Tom and Jeff were both born, but she couldn't have any more children, so they decided to take a foster child and bring it up with the other babies. When they'd had me about a year they adopted me legally, so I'm an Allbright, just like the other two."

"Where was the children's home?"

"In Bristol, I think. My real parents must have left Cornwall."

"Lyd!" The boys and Collie were coming back along

the quay on the other side of the little harbor. "Come on!"

"I must go. We have to help," Lyd explained. "I'm glad I've met you, Saul."

"So am I, Lyd Pratt-Platt-Allbright," Saul said, smiling at her. "See you tomorrow. I'll show you all that beach, if you like."

"Oh, will you? That would be kind."

"Glad to. All my friends are in Newlyn or Penzance, and it's rather dull here without young people. I went to school in Penzance by bus, but I've left now. You needn't go back by the road. There's a path that cuts up near the quay, and it brings you out right by the cottage."

Lyd said good-bye, rejoined her brothers, and pointed out the path between the rocks and the high foxgloves. She was happy, for she had made a friend—a friend who might be interesting. What was it like to live there in that almost deserted cove, working with boats and helping an invalid father? Was that going to be his life? She looked forward to seeing Saul Treporth again and learning more about him.

Lyd helped her mother for an hour or two, but she was so sleepy that she started to get ready for bed at nine-thirty. There was a bathroom at the cottage, beyond the kitchen, and it was delicious to lie in the hot water and feel all the sticky heat wash away. Her bites glowed red, and they had been joined by a third on her kneecap, but they were soothed by some special stuff in a tube her mother had produced.

Her bedroom held only a big bed, a plain dresser, a chair, and a row of hooks, but Lyd liked it. From the window she looked into the last of the sunset, with the rising hillside dark against it.

She switched on the light—it was a pity, in a way, that the cottage didn't have old lamps—and drew her diary from her big shoulder bag. It was a thick red notebook, with "Very Strictly Private" printed in black on the cover. It was old-fashioned to keep a diary, and probably the girls at school would laugh if they knew. But Lyd had never had a really intimate friend, one she could tell her secret thoughts to, and the diary was a way of expressing herself. It was easier to write than to talk, anyway.

She didn't feel so sleepy anymore, so she crouched on the bed, wrote the date at the top of a page, and then began to scribble quickly.

> This has been a strange day, and parts of it were awful. The journey was a nightmare. I do so hate to be cooped up in a car. I can stand it for an hour or two, but it took so long to get to Cornwall. I wonder why I feel like that? I wish I weren't scared of so many things. I wish I could ask someone else, someone of my own age, if they feel the same. I thought I'd grow out of it, but I haven't. There are so many things I hate and fear. The car, of course, and I'm still a bit afraid of the dark. And I'm scared of thunder, and being laughed at, and not being loved enough by anyone. And the future. I'm scared of Dad losing his job, and of my having to leave school and take some awful dull job just so I'm earning my living. School hasn't always been so good (plenty of things to be scared of there), but at least it's familiar, and I love working hard, and I do so want to go to a university. Yet I'll feel guilty if I do, perhaps because Dad and Mother have done so much for me already, and I'd hate to be a burden.
>
> Even though I felt so terrible in the car, it was wonderful, in a way, to be in Cornwall—until we were coming down the lane. What happened then I don't know. I've never felt like that in my life before. What do they call it? Being possessed. I felt possessed by some force

. . . just for a few seconds. But I can't talk about it again, or even write about it very well.

There is a young man here called Saul Treporth. Saul! What a strange biblical name. I don't know why, but I felt different with him, not shy and on my guard, as I usually am with new people. I even told him more about the adoption than I ever have to anyone before. Maybe he is the kind of person one can talk to.

"Aren't you in bed, Lyd?" her mother's voice demanded and Lyd jumped guiltily, thrusting her diary under the pillow.

"Just going, Mother."

Mrs. Allbright waited until she lay down, then kissed her. "Good night, love. Sleep well."

After Tom and Jeff had gone to bed, Mr. and Mrs. Allbright sat in the living room, tiredly silent. Then she said, "I wish I knew what all that was about—Lyd having nightmares or something in the lane."

"It was nothing," her husband said abruptly. "You know Lyd. She's always had strange moods, and she doesn't like the car. Oh, she never says so. She hasn't for years. I don't know much about psychology, but I've always thought most of her troubles were caused by the fact that she was with her parents when they died."

"You may be right, although she was only two. And she minds being adopted, I'm afraid."

"She doesn't need to. I feel about her exactly as if she were my own child. Why should she mind *now*, after all these years?"

"Perhaps she always did mind, and she's grown more thoughtful lately. She's growing up, though she hasn't got very far with it yet. In some ways she's young for her age. But you know, she did look and sound very strange as we came down the lane. That's what really worries me."

"She was too hot, that's all."

"But she said she was *cold*."

"Oh, forget it! She'll be fine after a day or two. She met that boy and seemed to like him. She'll swim with him and explore."

"We'll all swim," said Mrs. Allbright more cheerfully. "I used to love it, but there's not been much chance the last few years."

They put out the lights and climbed the stairs as softly as possible.

The boys were already deeply asleep, but Lyd was not. She was conscious of the silence, broken only by the distant, soft sound of the sea and the last call of a bird. She heard her parents come upstairs, but knew nothing of the conversation they had just finished. It might have comforted her to know that they understood her feelings. She felt so alone and so deeply convinced that her terrors were unique.

I'm a coward! she told herself, tossing restlessly. It had never occurred to her that she was, in fact, brave, because she went on uncomplainingly no matter how she felt. Some things she had done so that the boys would not think her a hopeless fool and be ashamed of her. She had learned to swim only because Tom had dropped her into the deep end of the swimming pool and then had swum beside her until she found out how.

Why be scared of that lane on a hot August day, when there was nothing there to do any harm? It was beautiful, fringed with ferns and flowers. Perhaps there was a body in the wood. Could that be it? But why should she know?

I shall have to walk along the lane tomorrow, she thought. Have to. Maybe Saul will be with me and then I'll feel safe. That cold thing couldn't happen again.

After that, she drifted happily into the waking dreams that her solitary nature found comforting—dreams in which she was never scared of anything, in which she was a success, doing heroic things and even writing a real book that was published. In the dreams she was beautiful and admired by everyone. She had boy friends and sometimes danced all night. She was wondering whether Saul could dance as she fell asleep.

CHAPTER THREE

A Strange Mystery

In the morning it was misty early, but by the time all
the jobs were done the sun was hot and the sky was blue.
They all went down to the Cove, where Saul was sitting on
a wall with his swimming things beside him.

"I've been given the day off," he said smiling, after he
had been introduced to Mr. and Mrs. Allbright. "My
father says it's time I had a break. He has his better days,
when he can more or less manage."

"I hear he had an accident," Mr. Allbright remarked.
"Will he recover properly after a time?"

Saul's face was very grave as he led the way by a rough
path to the sandy beach, which was tucked in beneath a
lower section of cliff. "Not entirely, I'm afraid. But the
doctors think he may improve a good deal more." Then
he changed the subject, telling them about tides and
currents.

Lyd listened, scrambling close at his heels. He wore a
bright blue shirt that made his skin look even more suntanned than it had the day before. Saul was not handsome, but he looked healthy and intelligent, and she
loved the way he moved, so easily and swiftly.

They all undressed behind high rocks, and they swam
together for quite a time. Tom and Jeff splashed and

chased each other through the clear water, but Saul stayed close to Lyd, though it was evident that he was a fine swimmer. She felt suddenly happy, feeling the salt water cool on her body, and the agonies and uneasy thoughts of the previous day began to seem unreal. Looking upward as she floated on her back, she caught a glimpse of a cottage on a high part of the cliff.

"Oh, there's another cottage!" she said. "Does anyone live there?"

"Yes, an artist lives there," Saul explained. "A Mrs. Barstow. You'll meet her soon, I expect."

After a time Mr. Allbright, Tom, and Jeff decided to go and speak to Saul's father about renting a boat, and Mrs. Allbright also dressed and went back to Tamarisk Cottage. Saul and Lyd stayed on, lying on the sand, hearing the sound of the sea.

"They're nice, your folks," said Saul. "Ordinary. What's your father's job?"

"He's an electrician in a factory," Lyn told him. "It isn't a very secure job at the moment. They've been getting rid of a lot of workers. If we hadn't been offered the cottage very cheaply, we couldn't have come here."

Saul nodded. There was little money in his family, too.

"What kind of school do you go to?" he asked.

"Oh, a very big school in Bristol. There are nine hundred students."

"And what are you going to do when you leave school?"

Lyd frowned, staring at the dazzling sea.

"I might write books." She wanted to impress him, so she spoke with more confidence than usual. "I always do well in English, but I'm a fool over figures. What'll you be now that you've left school? Not a fisherman?" Already she was realizing that Saul was a thoughtful kind of person, and probably clever.

"Never a fisherman!" he said savagely. "I've seen . . .

heard. . . . It's no life. I'd like to be a doctor or a scientist. I want to do good things, find out how to help people. Only it will take years—college and all that."

She turned to look at him. His brown face was half buried in his curved arm and his voice was strained.

"And *can* you? Go to college, I mean?"

"I'm going," he said. "But not until next year. I took my last exams this summer, and I'm sure as anyone can be that I've done well. Since I'm going to have to wait a year, I've found a job in Penzance that will bring in some money. An office job, probably boring and certainly not well paid, but it will help. That's not until the end of September, for I plan to help here as long as the season lasts. Then, when winter comes, I'll keep on studying during the dark evenings. I'll tell you something funny, Lyd Allbright. I might be going to Bristol University."

Lyd jumped. The thought flashed through her mind that he might not be just a holiday friend. Maybe one day they would meet again.

"Yes," Saul went on. "I put down for Exeter or Bristol. They're two of the nearest, and I didn't feel I could go as far as Manchester or Liverpool. I've had interviews for both. I'm in at one of them if I get all the good passes I need. All that has been quite easy, and I think I'll get the marks. But . . . well, you can see it's difficult. I've had to fight with my conscience. The way things are at home. . . . And it will be years before I'm properly qualified and really earning."

Lyd then sat up. Here, incredibly, was someone with the same problem as her own. Well, maybe there were plenty of young people in this boat, but she had not talked to them. Most of the girls in her class were better off than she was. Surprise made her speak quickly:

"Oh, Saul! I feel exactly like that. I think I can do it, too, and I *want* to. I want it more than anything. But I keep on thinking maybe I ought to start earning. It's even worse for me, because I'm adopted."

"I don't see that that makes any difference," Saul said judicially. "You're their girl. Do they *want* you to stay on at school?"

"Mother does. Well, she says so. But I haven't really been able to discuss it. I'm scared to try. I don't know about Dad. He says a lot of things against college students, how they waste public money with protests and sit-ins, things like that."

"I've discussed it a little," said Saul. "In fact, I insisted at one point that I was giving up the whole idea. But my people really want me to go to college. Dad's keen on learning and having good qualifications, something he never had. But . . . I suppose every young person feels guilty about something."

Lyd lay back on the sand. *Did* they? She felt as if a door were beginning to open.

"I thought I was the only one," she mumbled.

Saul laughed and jumped up, then took her hand and pulled her to her feet.

"Come and swim again in that pool left by the tide. It's too fine a day for problems."

Lyd had an old watch. She looked at it when she was dressed and was surprised to find that the morning had gone. The time had come to go back and help with lunch.

"Let's go somewhere this afternoon," suggested Saul, as they walked back to the Cove. "I'll take you to see the standing stones, the Merry Maidens and the Pipers of Boleigh. It isn't far. You passed them in the car."

Lyd nodded, remembering. The Pipers were two tall stones standing up in fields a short distance apart, and the Maidens had been in another field on the left. She had read about them in the Cornish book, so had looked for them to keep her mind off the car. They were old, old stones.

That would mean going up the lane, but if Saul was with her it would probably be all right. Well, she had promised herself that she'd go, and today she felt much braver.

"I'll meet you at two o'clock by the inn," said Saul.

And he did. After lunch she found him there sitting on the grass, waiting. They started to walk up the lane side by side, but they sometimes had to crouch against a bank as cars came by, often traveling too fast, toward the Cove.

"Trelonyan Cove may not be used by fishing boats," said Lyd. "But plenty of people come."

"In summer they do. It's different in winter, though people do still come on fine days. Last winter, going to school, I walked up to the top of this lane in the dark, and it was dark again when I got off the bus on the way home."

Lyd shivered suddenly. Walk the lane in the dark? Even on this brilliant summer afternoon it was shadowy. But it was beautiful, she told herself again, stopping to look at a flower she didn't know. She could hear the stream, but could not see it yet. How far was the cold place?

She walked more and more slowly, and Saul looked at her in slight surprise. It must be near now; the banks were lower and she could see into the wood.

And then it happened again. Lyd was cold, so cold, and lost and scared.

Suddenly she was aware of Saul's voice sounding urgently in her ear:

"What's up, Lyd? What is it? You nearly got run over by that car."

"Car? I didn't see one." She was sweating, but dead

cold and breathless. "There's something in the wood," she added, before she could stop herself.

Saul did not laugh. His thin brown face was serious and anxious, as well as very puzzled. "Oh, come on, Lyd!" he protested. "Something in the wood? There is not. It's just a wood."

There was a slight opening in the trees, as if there had once been a path. All Lyd really wanted to do was to run, but she stood still, her face dappled by the shadows of the leaves.

"I thought. . . . Look, I felt the same way yesterday when we passed this place in the car. Dad was angry, but I. . . . Are you *sure* there isn't anything?"

Saul took her hand. His fingers were warm and firm. "Well, I don't think so. Come and see. Only be careful, because there are a lot of nettles and the ground's rough."

Lyd allowed herself to be drawn into the trees, though every step was an effort. Already she was deeply regretting having spoken; she should have hidden her feelings and walked on. It was *silly!* He would think her a baby, not a sensible girl of sixteen. Humiliation began to be stronger than fear.

Saul led her all the way to the tangled bank of the stream, which tumbled down rapidly toward the Cove. There really was nothing, except a lot of nettles and loose stones and sunlight falling in a shifting, sparkly way through the leaves.

"No bodies, no ghosts," he said.

"I thought there was . . . something. I'm sorry, Saul. Forget it."

Saul was silent. He was Cornish and had inherited a feeling that there was more in the world than could be seen, but he wasn't going to admit it.

"Let's go on to the standing stones," said Lyd.

They walked on quickly, neither of them saying much. Lyd thought he was probably regretting the friendship that had been growing so rapidly. She couldn't blame him. But there was nothing she could say to explain her strange reactions. She didn't understand them herself.

They reached one of the Pipers through a cabbage field, then climbed a stile and walked through a herd of cows to the ring of ancient stones called the Merry Maidens. Lyd was scared of cows, but that seemed like nothing after her feeling in the lane. Besides, she had disgraced herself enough.

She sat on one of the flatter stones and looked around. "They're terribly old, aren't they? Prehistoric, the book said. There are a lot of theories about them, but no one really knows why they were put here."

Saul looked at her curiously as she sat there, small and dark-haired in her short green dress. He had never cared much for girls, but this Lyd Allbright fascinated him. She was puzzling as well. She was not scared of the stones at all, although he had never liked passing them alone when he was younger. Old things had an atmosphere about them.

"What book?" he asked, after a moment.

"Oh, one about Cornwall I borrowed from the library last week."

"Did it tell you anything about Trelonyan?" Saul queried.

"No, nothing. The name wasn't in the index, and there wasn't a word in the text. It told about the stones, and then went on to describe Lamorna and Porthcurno."

"Well, come on. Let's go back. We could swim again, if you like. In the harbor, why not? You swim very well, so it'll be quite safe."

Lyd followed him across the field and over the stile.

Words trembled on her tongue, and she tried to force herself to keep silent. But she had to ask.

"Is there . . . another way back? Not down the lane."

"Yes, there is," Saul told her matter-of-factly. "A narrow path, very tangly and overgrown, on the other side of the stream, It comes out near our cottage. But you can't let yourself get nightmares about the lane, can you? I mean, you can't avoid it for two weeks."

She had nightmares already, but pride won. "I'll go back down the lane," she said.

Cars were going both ways, and it took quite a while to reach the "cold place." When they did, Lyd stopped and stared into the wood. Gradually she saw something forming . . . a shadow among the trees. It was a cottage built of gray stone, an old cottage, rather rundown, but lived in. Things showed vaguely in the windows: a plant, a chair back. And there were shadows on top of shadows, like damp marks on the stones. She saw a garden also, an orderly one with plants growing in rows, and a ghostly lavender bush.

"Lyd!"

"There's a cottage," she said. "With a garden. An old garden. The lavender bush is huge."

"There's nothing." Saul was holding her arm, trying to draw her on down the lane.

"But I saw it, Saul, like a shadow among the trees. Kind of gauzy, misty, but clear enough. It's gone now."

"You couldn't have seen what isn't there."

No, she couldn't, could she? And once more she had made a fool of herself in front of Saul.

He took his hand from her arm and walked a few steps into the wood. "There are all these nettles. That does mean, I think, there might once have been a house here.

And look at these loose stones." His tone was calm, but he was frowning.

Lyd was herself again, angry, proud, and ashamed. Now she only wanted to get away from the place. The lane, so far, seemed all right, except for that one spot.

"I'm sorry," she said brusquely. "I won't be such a fool again. I shouldn't have said anything. I must have imagined it."

"But why should you?"

"I do imagine things. My father and mother get mad at me if they know. They say I have to live life as it is, and they're right. I don't expect there was a cottage there." After a pause she added, "Saul, could we ask? Someone might know if there ever was one."

"There's no one to ask," Saul said quickly. "My family came from Newlyn, remember, and the Pendennises came from St. Ives two years ago. The Clarks aren't even Cornish. Everyone else has gone."

"I really am sorry." Was she going to lose this new friend, who seemed somehow very important? The habit of secrecy should have held. Lyd felt very much alone.

"We'll both forget it," Saul said. "Everything has an old feeling around here. Maybe you picked up something, though I don't see why *you* should. Sometimes in the dark I thought . . ." He didn't go on to describe his reactions to this country in the early morning and late on a winter afternoon. He was going to be a doctor or a scientist.

They began to walk very quickly on down the lane toward the Cove.

CHAPTER FOUR

Lyd Alone

Lyd tried to talk naturally. She told him a little about school, about their home in Bristol, and how Collie had come to them from Wales as a small fluffy pup. At the point where the lane went up to the cottage she stopped.

"Saul, I'm not going swimming again."

Saul stopped, too. "Why not. Don't you feel well?"

Just then a woman came out of the store and crossed toward them. She was middle-aged and wore slacks and a yellow blouse. She was carrying a basket of groceries.

"Hello, Saul!" she said.

"Good afternoon, Mrs. Barstow," answered Saul.

"I see you have a new friend."

"Yes, it's Lyd Allbright. She's staying with her family at Tamarisk Cottage."

"How do you do, Lyd?" Mrs. Barstow smiled in a friendly way. "I heard you'd all arrived, and I believe I caught a glimpse of you swimming this morning. I must visit Tamarisk Cottage soon and meet your parents."

"A nice woman," said Saul, when they were alone again. "She's the artist I mentioned this morning. She came to live here in the spring and spends most of her time painting. She held a show of her work in one of the deserted buildings in July. Her pictures are kind of impressions, very interesting. She sold quite a number of them."

"She has a kind face," said Lyd. "But her eyes are sad. She seemed a very alive kind of person. I never met an artist before."

"She's alive all right," Saul agreed. "And kind, too. She often goes to talk to my father, and they get on very well. It's good for him; he usually doesn't unbend to strangers. You're right about the sadness, too. Her husband left her last winter, so she came here to live alone and paint."

"*Left* her? How awful! Why?" Lyd was shocked. How dreadfully unsafe life could be.

"I don't know any details. You wouldn't think anyone would want to leave her, but I suppose it does happen," Saul said slowly. "She just told Mrs. Clark her husband had left her and that she had to start again. She has two daughters, both married."

They stood looking at each other for a moment; then Saul said abruptly, "Well, if you won't come swimming I'd better get home and do some work. Dad can walk all right with his crutches, but he gets fussed if there are too many people wanting boats."

Now that he was leaving her, Lyd wished she had agreed to go swimming again.

"Saul, you won't tell anyone? My dad would be furious with me if he knew. Please don't tell. I won't be such a fool again."

"No, of course I won't." But Saul looked troubled. "Would your father really be mad at you? He looks very sensible and kind. He might not understand, but maybe you should—"

Lyd stirred up the loose stones with the toe of her sandal, not looking at him. "Do you tell your parents everything?"

That was hitting below the belt. No, Saul didn't. He had gone to great lengths to keep his feelings hidden during the difficult times that had followed his father's accident.

"Not always," he admitted.

"Do you think most young people tell things?"

Saul was honest and clear-minded, and he knew that they didn't. Even the best parents in the world didn't seem able to remember what it was like to be young. And Lyd wasn't at all like her adoptive parents, so perhaps that put up an extra barrier.

"No," he said. "But I can see it's a good idea to tell them if you can."

"Well, I can't, and that's the end of it. I did say it was cold and awful in the lane, and Dad *was* mad. And what more is there to tell? I thought I saw a cottage—"

"If you did, why was it so terrifying?" Saul asked suddenly. "I mean, I know it's strange to think you saw something like that, but a ghostly cottage . . . it couldn't bite you."

In fact, it had looked like a nice cottage, shabby and ordinary.

"I don't know. It was as if . . . someone else was afraid."

Saul went off rather quickly, and Lyd climbed the lane to Tamarisk Cottage. She climbed very slowly, a little lulled by the drowsy heat of afternoon. Halfway up she sat on the bank among the foxgloves and bees—and the bees, busy with their own concerns, took no notice of her. She felt sleepy and sad and, in the end, she did fall asleep, with her head resting against an outcrop of stone.

When she awoke, her father, Tom, and Jeff were coming up the lane, laughing and talking. They carried some of their fishing gear and the baskets, and in the baskets were a great many shining fish. Lyd quickly slid off the bank, blinking, and wondering if she had dreamed the whole strange afternoon.

"What are you doing here, Lyd?" asked Tom. "Waiting for us?"

"Yes," said Lyd. "Fish for supper?"

"And for breakfast. We had a good afternoon."

Lyd fell into step with them, relieved that they didn't seem to notice anything wrong. But she was suddenly filled with a feeling of desolation. These three big, fair people seemed united in a cheerful companionship, while she felt separate, and hated it. Yet, she thought, Tom and Jeff did have secrets from their parents, too. On the surface their lives were easy and open. They moderately enjoyed school, at least the more practical part of it. They did well at games, eagerly followed the careers of professional footballers, and sometimes of pop singers, and were too equable and peace-loving ever to get into real trouble.

But when Jeff *was* in any trouble at school he did everything he could to keep it from his father, and when Tom had gone out with his first girl, he never said a word. Lyd only knew because she'd seen them on the grassy heights near the Clifton Suspension Bridge, and Tom had sworn her to secrecy.

"You know Dad would say I was too young."

He still went out with the girl; she was a nice, pretty girl of fourteen. Sometimes they just went for a walk, but if he had money he took her to a movie. Lyd felt pleased to be in his confidence and had never tried to advise him. How could she, when, although nine months older, she had had no experience? But one would never have thought *now* that there were any secrets, even such mild ones.

Jeff was speaking, breaking into her thoughts. "How did you know we wouldn't come up the other path, Lyd?"

"I—I suppose I didn't." She noticed that her father was carrying some bottles and cans in a paper shopping bag.

"We went to buy some Coke and lemonade."

You could see the inn and post office over the top of the bank where she had been sitting. She laughed. "Well, I was in a good place to see."

Then she felt worse than ever, because it was a lie. Only they mustn't know. She couldn't spoil their happiness and make everyone annoyed with her. Violently she wanted to belong. Usually she did, so why did she feel so out of things now? It was as if she had been in another world.

Mrs. Allbright said she had had a peaceful afternoon. Mrs. Clark had come up and asked her to go down to the Trelonyan Arms for a cup of tea, and on her return she had sat in the cottage garden, enjoying the sunshine and the flowers.

Soon the whole cottage was filled with the delectable smell of fish frying. Lyd set the table, peeled the potatoes, and tried to be her usual self. But the feeling of isolation had grown worse, and she seemed to have forgotten what she was usually like.

All the same, the fish was delicious and she made a fair meal.

"What's the matter, Lyd?" her mother asked, as they washed the dishes. "You're very quiet."

"Nothing."

"There must be something. Didn't you enjoy yourself with Saul? Don't you like him? He seems very nice, with such pleasant manners."

"Yes, I like him very much." That was true, but she felt a little pain at her heart when she thought that Saul might be having second thoughts about her.

"Do you have a headache then? The sun was very hot."

"*No.*"

"All right, love. Don't bite my head off."

Lyd felt like crying and quickly went out into the garden with Collie. She threw his ball and Collie eagerly ran after it and brought it back. Although he was now two years old he often still acted like a puppy.

Lyd wondered suddenly if Collie would mind the lane. Next time she would take him with her and see how he reacted. People said that dogs were scared of ghosts. Next time . . . Well, there would have to be another time. She couldn't stay shut up in the cottage for nearly two whole weeks, and she couldn't stamp herself as a hopeless coward by taking the path Saul had mentioned. He would know, even if he wasn't with her, for it was near his home.

Besides, a feeling was growing that scared her very much. She had to know more: just why was it like that in the lane, and why did she think she had seen a cottage that might have been there long ago. Long ago . . . How long? Twenty years? Fifty years? Perhaps a hundred or even two hundred years ago?

Tom came strolling out and joined in the game with the dog. Lyd felt better, more like herself. Tom was her brother. If no one else bothered that she was adopted, why should she? Probably they would never remember, if she didn't remind them. When she was a foster child they must have been paid for having her, but after she was legally adopted, the money stopped coming. A girl at school had said that once. Lyd didn't hate many people, but she had always rather hated that girl.

In bed at last, Lyd felt more alone than she ever had. She felt an almost overpowering desire to go to her mother and cling to her, as she had sometimes done when she was little. She longed to feel loved and wanted and safe. But she wasn't safe. Maybe no one ever was. And Mrs. Barstow was a *mother,* but she had had to start life again all alone. It might be easier to bear things when you were quite old, but Mrs. Barstow's eyes were definitely sad, even though she was a successful artist and gave that impression of being extra alive.

Bees and foxgloves and scattered stones in a wood. . . . Saul might already be asleep in that cottage behind the derelict lofts.

The bed felt very hot . . . the little room was hot. Lyd began to long to be outdoors, sitting on a bank in the darkening evening. She thought she could climb out of the window quite easily, for the bathroom roof jutted out just below, and then there was a good, thick pipe.

But she turned to her diary instead. She drew the gay cotton drapes, and switched on the light. Then she began to scribble, trying to write down her experiences of the day. It wasn't easy and took a long time; then she went on writing, almost doodling down her thoughts.

I hope Saul will still be friends. I never had a real boy friend before. . . . Now I come to think of it, I have never had a real *friend.* I like everything about him. I like his looks, and the way he moves, and his Cornish voice. I like the way he talked to me when we were sitting on the beach. He has plenty of troubles and problems, but he's so sane and clever. I'd hate him to think me a fool. Maybe he didn't, but he *was* puzzled.

Well, that makes two of us. As he said, why should it
be me? If there is something to feel and see in that lane,
one would think Saul would know, for he *is* Cornish
and he half admitted it's strange country. Well, of
course, I may be Cornish, too. Can I be psychic? I've
never shown any signs of it before. I don't think I like
that idea. I'll forget it.

But whatever it is, I'm going to face it. I'm going to
find out, even if I never mention it to Saul again. I
have the feeling it's something I can't avoid, that I'm
meant to know it. Maybe that's silly, for it was surely
just chance that gave us this cottage in Trelonyan. I'm
scared, but I'm curious. Only I hope, hope, hope that
Saul will still see me. Bristol University . . . fancy! He
might be in my life for years, unless he goes to Exeter.
I think I could learn a lot from Saul. I certainly have a
lot to learn. In a few years I could be married, with
children of my own. Will they have secrets, too, and
feel all alone? I hope not, but how does one stop it?
Each person really is alone, I suppose, but some people
never think of it, and maybe some don't even mind.
I mind. But if I'm alone then I'll do the best I can.

Lyd thrust her diary back into her scarlet shoulder bag
and turned out the light. Those dream children were still
far in the future, and all that mattered was tomorrow.

CHAPTER FIVE

A Growing Vision

In the morning Saul arrived before the Allbrights had finished breakfast. They were late because it was such a gloomy day, with mist swirling around the cottage and obscuring the Cove.

Lyd's heart leaped when she saw him. He had come to her and not waited until she went down in search of him. Then she saw that he was carrying two large plastic shopping bags.

"I'm going into Penzance to do the shopping," he explained. "Things are much cheaper there, even after paying the bus fare, and one has more choice. The bus gets me back to the top of the lane at twelve-thirty, Lyd, so I'll see you this afternoon."

"I don't know what you'll do in this weather," said Mrs. Allbright.

Saul laughed. "The mist will lift. By afternoon I think it will be hot and sunny again. Now I must fly, or I'll miss the bus."

"You should have a bicycle," remarked Mr. Allbright.

"I did have one once. But in the end it was old enough

to be really unsafe. Besides, the hills make it difficult. It's no joke pushing up from Newlyn or Mousehole."

Lyd watched Saul go with regret. She would have liked to be in a town, among a lot of people, pushing her way around a supermarket, taking brightly colored cans off the shelves. And Penzance had looked interesting, with its big harbor, the great church on the hill, and a hint of narrow old lanes and attractive houses. Anything would have been better than the brooding, misty silence of Trelonyan. Maybe Saul would have asked her to go, if she hadn't still been sitting at the breakfast table. At least he had come, and she was going to see him that afternoon. Perhaps her desperate wish was going to be answered, and he wasn't intending to avoid her.

When the jobs were done, Mr. Allbright, Tom, and Jeff went down to fish off the quay. Collie wanted to accompany them, but he obeyed the order to stay behind. Collie was not a roving dog, in spite of his Welsh ancestry. He was perhaps conditioned by two years of living in Bristol. He was also obedient, so he stayed at the cottage.

"They're rather scared to have him running loose down there, though I doubt if there'll be many cars this morning," said Mrs. Allbright.

When Lyd went into the garden to pick roses, Collie was at her side. The roses, pink, red, and yellow, were festooned with shining drops of moisture and smelled all the sweeter. While Lyd arranged them in blue vases, her mother made pastry for a pie.

"I wish the blackberries were ripe," she said. "There are going to be millions of them later."

The Allbrights had brought a transistor radio with them, so there was music and then a story that Mrs. Allbright seemed to be enjoying. Lyd was glad, because it was such a strain trying to sound like her usual self. She did feel more "belonging" this morning, but the thought of what she meant to do hung over her. There seemed to be no way out, and that was strange.

Perhaps it was courage and curiosity combined, as well as the urgent need to see Saul again before the afternoon. She had never before in her life felt a real, deep longing to be in another person's company. It was an entirely new experience, both painful and pleasurable.

I believe I *am* growing up, Lyd said to herself.

At a quarter to twelve, the mist still obscured the scene, but there were signs that the sun was trying to break through. Lyd went to put on her red hooded jacket and fetched Collie's leash.

"Mother," she said, "I'm going to meet Saul off the bus."

"What a good idea! You can help him carry the things. But be careful on that narrow road, Lyd, and keep Collie on the leash."

"I'll be careful," promised Lyd. For just a moment she hesitated, wondering if she could tell her mother about the strange thing in the lane. She certainly couldn't bring herself to speak about Saul; their friendship was too nebulous yet, too much a private matter. But if she tried to explain about the ghostly cottage, her mother would be worried, and she would certainly tell her father.

Lyd went out quickly and set off down the lane from the house. It was really quite warm in spite of the clinging mist, and she didn't need the jacket, except to keep out the damp. She went over to the shop and bought some chocolate, and Mrs. Pendennis seemed delighted to see her.

"Well, my dear!" she cried. "Are you enjoying being here? I hear that you and Saul are great friends already."

Lyd wasn't used to country ways, for she had lived all

her life in a city. How had Mrs. Pendennis "heard"? And would she hear equally quickly if the friendship was over?

"Oh, yes," she said casually. "I'm going to meet him off the bus now."

Mrs. Pendennis knew that Saul Treporth made shopping expeditions into Penzance, and she didn't resent the fact. It was natural, when the family was so short of money. Her own goods weren't as cheap as those in a supermarket and she didn't have the selection. They bought plenty of things from her, anyway, especially in bad weather.

"I'm sure he'll be glad to see you, my dear," she said.

Lyd hoped she was right.

The corner where the inn and store stood seemed familiar and safe. Ahead lay the tree-arched lane, curving between its high banks. There were no cars around now, only a butcher's van. After a few moments' hesitation Lyd walked on, stopped occasionally by Collie, who found plenty of interesting scents on the way. His fur was soon spangled with drops of moisture and his tail waved with pleasure. *Collie* wasn't scared of the lane, but how would he behave when they reached the "cold place"?

Lyd was glad of the stops, which gave her an excuse to gaze into the tangled growth of the bank. Behind it lay a whole secret world: a scarlet and black ladybird on a shining leaf, ants going busily about their lives, a bee apparently asleep in a foxglove bell, and so many flowers and plants. It was annoying that she knew so few names, and she resolved to ask Saul to teach her. That would be a safer subject than ghostly cottages—if, of course, he knew the names himself. Otherwise, maybe she could go and look at a flower book in the Penzance library.

Thinking thus, she went on again and, in the absence

of traffic, made rapid progress. She hauled at Collie's leash and made him resist the next few scents. The world was so obscured and dreamlike in the mist that she reached the "cold place" even before she expected it. But she was ready, tensed and alert, and in a strange way less scared than formerly. The atmosphere was eerie, but perhaps Collie's presence was a safeguard. The coldness, when it came, was milder than on the other occasions, even though she had her usual violent longing to run at the first feeling of possession. That was the word that came into her mind again.

Collie looked up at her in a puzzled way and brushed damply against her bare legs. He was troubled, but he wasn't scared. He had sensed something in her, but he was still happy enough, his tail erect. The "cold place" meant nothing to him.

The mist was definitely parting and dispersing, and the sky was faintly blue above the leafy branches. A glitter of sun touched the road ahead, but Lyd was staring into the wood, where once again she saw, hazy in the moving mist, but growing clearer than before, the small stone cottage, with its door open upon a glimpse of old, dark furniture. The garden was there, too; she could see the rows of plants stretching in a ghostly way between the trees. She could see the big lavender bush quite clearly, and other bushes. An old woman was bent over one of them, gathering long green spikes.

The old woman wore a voluminous dark dress and a white apron. Close to her feet was a cat, not a black cat, but a well-grown tabby. Both woman and cat were perfectly visible, but Lyd could see through them. She blinked, but they were still there like a dim picture hanging in the air, yet with their feet on the ground.

The cat came slowly toward the lane, but Collie took no

notice at all. He hated cats, but now he only wanted to go
on. He was tugging at his leash and looking up at Lyd
inquiringly. How very strange that he couldn't see or
sense the cat, which had now reached the lane! The cat
was a handsome beast, with shining fur and amber eyes.

Slowly he lay down and rolled over, in the way cats do
when pleased or contented. She could see the rough road
and a fallen leaf through him. Again she blinked, but he
was still there, showing a streaky white stomach and
waving one paw beguilingly.

Lyd had quite forgotten fear in her fascination with
the cat. She actually leaned over to see if she could touch
him, but suddenly he was gone and so was the cottage.
She walked on, talking to herself.

"Whoever saw the ghost of a cottage and the ghost of a
cat? And such a pretty cat. I *must* be imagining the
whole thing. It wasn't really frightening that time. Of
course there was the old woman as well, but I only saw
her for a moment, because I was watching the cat. She
looked nice and as if she liked her garden. Maybe *she*
wasn't scared this morning."

If the whole thing wasn't just some kind of illusion,
Lyd had arrived at the point where she could understand
that the terror she felt in the lane was not her own, but
someone else's. She had already known that the day before, but not so clearly as she did now.

Had something awful happened to the old woman?
She looked so safe in her garden among her plants.

Lyd saw that she had reached the top of the lane. She
leaned against the signpost, pushing back her hood and
unfastening the jacket. One arm of the signpost pointed
down to Trelonyan Cove, one to St. Buryan and Land's
End, and the third to Newlyn and Penzance. From that

last direction the bus would come, but it wasn't due for another five minutes and might well be late. So she continued to muse.

If there had ever been a cottage it must have disappeared a long time ago, because a whole wood had grown up thickly and she had seen the gauzy picture against and among the tree trunks. Some trees grew quickly and others didn't, Lyd thought, but she knew hardly any by name. It was really awful to be so ignorant on country matters, and she would certainly have to learn. Just the same, call it fifty years, though it might be a lot more. That made it practically the Dark Ages to one side of Lyd's mind, although she knew perfectly well that in Britain you could go back two thousand years, and even a lot more. She thought about the Romans living where the modern city of Bath now stood. That alone was nearly two thousand years ago, and the Stone Age, the Bronze Age, the Iron Age and a good many other civilizations had come before that. Once she had visited an ancient burial mound high on the Cotswold Hills called Belas Knap. . . . Hadn't it been Neolithic?

Anyway, there was no need to think back so far. The old woman had looked ordinary enough. She had not been wearing a bonnet or a cap; she had had neat white hair pinned up on her head. Curiously, Lyd was sure of that, in spite of just one misty glimpse.

She heard the bus coming and her heart beat faster. Suddenly Saul was more important than the old woman and her cat. Would he be pleased to see her, or annoyed? Perhaps she shouldn't have come to meet him. She should have waited at home until he sought her out again.

The bus came slowly down into the leafy hollow and stopped. It was a green Western National bus, going on to St. Buryan and Porthcurno. Saul descended the steps carrying one bulging bag; then he turned to haul a second one after him. He seemed delighted to see Lyd, and her heart resumed a more normal beat.

"How nice of you, Lyd!" he said cheerfully. "I never thought you'd come. Did you walk along the lane? But you had your dog. No, this is too heavy for you to carry. I can manage both."

"It isn't. I may be small, but I'm strong. Oh, well, take a few things out of that one. You're going to lose them if you don't." Lyd firmly extracted a huge pack of detergent, and another of cornflakes.

"We will go by the footpath today," Saul said. "It's a good deal quicker to our cottage, and you can let Collie off the leash. He'll like that."

The path was indeed very tangly, as though it weren't used much. It kept close to the far bank of the stream, and Lyd involuntarily glanced into the wood when they reached what she thought must be the point opposite the "cold place." Nothing at all happened. She just saw a wood, heavy with summer greenery.

Saul saw her turn her head. "Was it all right in the lane?" he asked. His voice was calm and gently inquiring, but Lyd flushed and hesitated. She longed to say airily, "Quite all right. Don't let's speak of it any more." But she couldn't deny the strange reality of the cottage, the old woman, and the cat, and all her resolutions were forgotten.

"I wasn't really scared," she temporized.

"You mean you saw it again?"

Lyd stopped and Saul thankfully put down the two heavy bags.

"Do you really want to hear?" she asked.

"Yes, if you saw anything. You have to tell someone, don't you?"

"I don't know. I didn't mean to, Saul. But, yes, I did see it, more clearly. There was an old woman in the garden, picking something, and a cat." Once started on her story, Lyd was in a hurry to go on, but Saul interrupted her.

"A cat? Didn't Collie go mad?"

Lyd stared after Collie, who was way ahead, looking for rabbits.

"Saul, he didn't *know*. He knew I was different, but he didn't see the cat, or sense it. And it came right out into the lane and rolled over. It had a lovely white stomach, but I could see the stones and a leaf through it. I wasn't at all scared, not after the first few moments, but of course I must be imagining it. If there really had been anything, Collie would have known."

Saul was frowning. "I would have thought so—if they were what people call ghosts."

"But do you believe in ghosts?"

"No-o. No, I don't. Only, maybe, in a—a certain feeling in old places. Come on. We'd better get these things home. Go on talking as we walk."

Lyd groped after words that would illuminate what she had seen.

"It was like seeing a movie on a screen made of gauze. Exactly like that. If the screen had been solid I would have seen it all more clearly, and without the trees, of course. They do get in the way. They weren't there, I'm sure, when the cottage was."

Saul seemed more disturbed than Lyd liked. His face was grave and troubled, and she wished she had said nothing. Once again she might have endangered their friendship.

"I shouldn't have told you," she muttered unhappily.

"Yes, you should. Have you ever had any experiences of this kind before?"

"No. Of course not. I don't understand it at all."

They soon reached the cottage where Saul lived. Lyd went in with him and met his father and mother for the first time. His mother was a pale, worried-looking woman with a soft, lilting voice. Mr. Treporth was sitting at the kitchen table, with his crutches propped up near by. He was small and dark, and Saul was very like him in features, though much better built. In a strange moment of awareness and grief, Lyd hoped that Saul would never look like that . . . so worn, thin, and old. Probably Mr. Treporth was often in pain.

Something was frying, which reminded Lyd that it was lunch time and she must go home quickly. By now the mist had gone, and the water was blue and the sun shining hotly. She took off her jacket as she hesitated on the doorstep.

"Good-bye, Saul."

"Why don't you come down this afternoon?" Saul asked. "There'll be tourists and plenty to do. How'd you like to help? We can take over from Dad."

"Oh, yes!" That was something practical she could do. Boats and fishing gear were real, and if it meant that Mr. Treporth could rest it would be worthwhile.

"See you later, then."

Saul did mean to go on being friends, and that was comforting, but during lunch Lyd still felt that awful remoteness from her family. It wasn't really difficult to tell Saul about strange, unlikely things, but it would be *impossible* to tell her family.

She imagined how Tom and Jeff would laugh, and how angry and distressed her father would be if she suddenly said, "I saw a ghostly cottage and a transparent cat rolling happily in the lane. Then everything disappeared."

No, she couldn't do it, but she couldn't forget what had happened, either. Whatever was happening, it had a deep significance and importance that could not be denied. Each time she learned more, or rather *saw* something more. Would the whole tale unfold? And, if it did, why to her?

"Lyd, are you sure you haven't a headache or a pain?" her mother asked, while they were washing the dishes.

"No, of course not. I'm fine." Lyd put all the assurance she could into her answer.

"You look all right, but I thought . . ." Mrs. Allbright didn't finish the sentence, and the moment the dishes were put away, Lyd went upstairs to comb her hair and put on lipstick. Lipstick made her feel and look a little more grown up.

She stared at herself in the mirror and thought that she did look all right, even a bit better than yesterday. Her eyes were bright, and her cheeks were pink. Maybe that was because she was spending the afternoon with Saul.

Mrs. Allbright watched her daughter hurry out of the cottage and turn toward the little path that went so steeply down to the Cove. She supposed that Lyd was happy enough, for she certainly seemed eager to help with the boats. If there was any trouble, it didn't seem to concern Saul Treporth, and that was a relief. It was time that Lyd made older friends and developed a little.

I wish I could really talk to her, Mrs. Allbright thought as she went to sit in the garden. Maybe that's the cry of all mothers, but I do feel so inarticulate. And when I try, she cuts me off at once.

But it was too fine an afternoon for worrying unduly. Mrs. Allbright sat sewing, reveling in the sunshine after the misty morning. After an hour or so she rose and leaned on the bank, gazing down at the Cove. In a few moments she picked out Lyd's figure as she helped Saul push out a boat. A lot of activity was going on down there, and much of it would mean money for the Treporths.

Already, in one way and another, the Allbrights were identifying themselves with Trelonyan Cove.

CHAPTER SIX

Another Friend

Two mainly very happy days passed. On the first of them Lyd helped Saul with the boats both morning and afternoon. The weather was glorious, and a lot of tourists and serious fishermen were out. Lyd was very suntanned already, and she wore her oldest clothes. Working with Saul made her feel at peace, and for the very first time in her life she was really at ease with another human being. Only an occasional thought of the ghostly cottage intruded, and sometimes she glanced inland, where the narrow valley, tree-filled, came down toward the Cove.

The Cove itself she still thought grim; nothing could make the harsh slopes to the east look attractive. But she hadn't much time for thinking, and her mother, walking down to speak to them after a visit to the store, said to herself, I've never seen Lyd look like this. She has a kind of glow. She really likes that young man.

That evening Lyd wrote in her diary:

It was a lovely day. Saul and I talked when we could, but we never once mentioned what happened in the lane yesterday. I have the feeling that this is just an interlude, and that something is hanging over me, something I'm not going to like, but that I have to face. And I'm scared. . . . When wasn't I scared of something? But the thing is there, and not even this happy, sunny day really made it disappear.

All the same, I did have many happy hours. I felt alive all over, with the sun on my skin, my feet bare some of the time, and my hands on ropes and boats.

I wish we could do it again tomorrow. I wish I didn't have to go out in the car, but Dad was hurt when I tried to get out of it. Parents! I suppose that is part of belonging, and it's what I want, isn't it? And yet it might just be a feeling of duty on his part. They'd probably be perfectly happy, just the four of them. But Mother has said I can sit in the front, and we aren't going very far. I suppose I do have to see more of Cornwall than just this corner, and I *want* to. I want several things at once. . . . I seem to be a really mixed-up kid. Yet I have the strange feeling that things may get clearer, that I'm on the right path now. And there's no sense in that.

Mrs. Clark had offered to have Collie for the day, so without their luggage and the dog, there was much more room in the car. Mrs. Allbright sat in the back with the boys, and Lyd took her place in front. She clasped her hands, held her breath, and looked the other way when they passed the "cold place." Even so, she felt something and barely repressed a shudder. However, once they were on the road to St. Buryan, with the rolling country stretching away into the distance, she felt better, and soon the great tower of the church was behind them. They went to Porthcurno, then on to Land's End, where the high cliffs dropped to the Atlantic Ocean. But the place was filled with far too many buses and tourists.

"There's no *atmosphere!*" complained Lyd. Then she wondered why she wanted atmosphere when there was already more than she could cope with around Trelonyan Cove.

"We'll go on to Cape Cornwall. I believe that's better," said Mr. Allbright. He didn't see anything wrong with people enjoying themselves in parties, even if they did leave litter, and Tom and Jeff agreed with him. But Mrs. Allbright understood what Lyd meant.

"It must be wonderfully exciting here during the winter," she said. "But in August it's just too crowded."

"It would be mighty cold in the winter," retorted her husband, but he turned the old car around and drove north to St. Just and Cape Cornwall.

The abandoned old tin mines near St. Just appealed to Lyd for some reason, and Cape Cornwall was certainly better than Land's End. She and the boys scrambled for some distance along the cliff path, and the juxtaposition of sunlight, warm grass and gorse, and the dark-blue sea made all her problems and secret fears seem unimportant.

They had tea in St. Ives, where there were a great many more tourists, and returned in the evening to Trelonyan. Going down the lane, Lyd shut her eyes, but felt the air change, or something in herself change, as they passed the gap in the bank that led into the wood. Maybe her mother saw her shoulders tense, for she put her hand out and touched her daughter.

"You all right, Lyd?" she asked.

"Of course I am," Lyd snapped, before she could stop herself, and her father protested at once.

"That's no way to speak to your mother," he said. "Don't spoil a happy day."

It was good to return to the tamarisk peace of the cottage, and in spite of those few sharp words, Lyd thought it really had been a happy day, a real family outing. Maybe she really belonged, after all, and was not different from the others. Perhaps she would not again be drawn into anything strange and difficult to explain.

But the very next afternoon, when she was wandering alone in the lower part of the lane, still within sight of the inn and the store, the cold feeling suddenly engulfed her. Lyd had decided to pick honeysuckle for the cottage on her way home, and she was quite happy and unconcerned when it came over her. She actually threw herself against the bank, as though something were surging past her. There were people, she felt, a crowd of people—and an overpowering feeling of fear.

She cowered and shivered when a hand touched her shoulder.

"Lyd! What is it, dear? Are you sick?"

It was Mrs. Barstow, her suntanned face wearing an expression of concern. She had propped her old bicycle against the bank and was bending over Lyd. In the large basket on the bicycle were paints and canvases, and a folding easel was strapped on behind.

Lyd blinked at her, still not quite back in the real world.

"I—I was getting out of the way," she stammered. "There were people, a big crowd of them. Everyone was so angry, and someone was afraid." Then she realized what she had said, and gasped and stopped. She had given herself away to a *stranger*.

"Come with me," Mrs. Barstow said calmly. "I'm going home for a cup of tea, and you look as if you need one. You've had a shock of some kind."

Lyd didn't want to go, but she hadn't the presence of mind, or the social aplomb, to refuse gracefully. She felt sick and still cold and somehow exposed.

She wished that Saul were somewhere around, but he had left her thirty minutes earlier to catch the bus into

Penzance, where he was going to see a former school friend. And Tom and Jeff were fishing and wouldn't be back until supper time.

"Come on, Lyd," urged Mrs. Barstow. "You'll like my cottage, and I'll be glad of your company."

She must be lonely. How awful that her husband had left her! And why did he when she was so nice? Why did people do terrible things to each other? Lyd walked slowly beside Mrs. Barstow, who pushed the bicycle. There was a path near the harbor that led up to the top of the headland, and like their own rough way to Tamarisk Cottage, it was festooned with foxgloves, red campion, and ferns.

Mrs. Barstow talked all the way, telling Lyd she was painting near Porthcurno. She had a pleasant voice, with a slight London accent.

Her cottage, which they could just glimpse from the sandy beach, was built of granite and was very much like Tamarisk Cottage, except that every wall was hung with paintings—in the living room, the tiny hallway, and even the kitchen. Lyd was fascinated and forgot some of her awkwardness and recent fear as she wandered around looking at them.

The pictures were impressions, but recognizable scenes in some cases. There was Trelonyan Cove, deserted and desolate, with a suggestion of storm. It looked just as grim and unfriendly as Lyd had always thought it. And there was another of the harbor from close to, with boats upturned and the derelict buildings suggested in dark grays. Someone who looked like Saul was leaning over a wall.

Mrs. Barstow left Lyd to wander until the kettle had boiled and she had made the tea. She buttered some muffins and produced chocolate cookies, and Lyd was invited to sit at the table.

"I think I see your brothers fishing from a boat," Mrs. Barstow remarked.

Lyd, on her way to the table, looked out the window and saw the boat. Life was so simple for Tom and Jeff, in spite of rows at school and first girl friends. They were always happy in each other's company, and there they were out on the calm blue water.

"Where's your father, Lyd?" Mrs. Barstow asked, as she handed her a cup of tea.

"Oh, I expect he's still cleaning the car and tinkering with the engine. He was just starting on it when I went out."

"I met your father and mother the day before yesterday. Did they tell you? I visited the cottage while you were helping Saul."

Lyd nodded. They had mentioned the visit, and she had received the impression that they didn't quite know how to take Mrs. Barstow, though her mother had said she was nice. Artists, and especially one deserted by her husband and living all alone, were not in their normal experience. Even Mr. Treporth was likely to meet more artists than the Allbrights, for Saul had said people often painted the Cove.

Lyd blushed a little at her thoughts. She felt tongue-tied and wished she'd never come.

But the tea was hot and sweet and she soon began to feel better, more at ease, although she was remembering that thing in the lane, not at the "cold place," but right down near the inn and the post office. She had felt people surging past—men mostly, she thought—and someone was afraid. It had been awful, but she tried not to think about it.

Mrs. Barstow waited until Lyd had drunk two cups of tea and eaten three muffins and a chocolate cookie; then she asked quietly, "What happened when I met you? There was no one there, Lyd."

Lyd gulped and half hated her. She wished herself miles away.

"I don't know what you mean," she muttered, using the time-honored words of self-protection. She realized that they sounded childish and sulky.

"Something had upset you. Why were you clinging to the bank like that?"

"I thought there was a car. You know how they swing around the bend."

"But there wasn't a car, and you dropped your honeysuckle and looked so scared," Mrs. Barstow persisted.

"Something stung me." Lyd gazed at her with enmity, and Mrs. Barstow looked calmly back.

"Lyd," she said, "I have two daughters. They are both married now, even the younger one, who is nineteen, but I know when young girls are scared, and you were."

Lyd glared, feeling hopelessly trapped. She might tell Saul when he came back. He had said he wouldn't be late; he was mainly going to borrow some books. Never, never would she tell Mrs. Barstow. And it was terrible if things were going to happen right down there, within sight of buildings and people. Her aloneness engulfed her. Suddenly she longed violently to be back in the streets of Bristol, where nothing uncanny ever happened.

"There was nothing."

Mrs. Barstow was silent for at least half a minute; then she said, "This is a strange place. I don't belong here, but I feel something. Cornwall always had an eerie feeling. You said you were getting out of the way, because there was a crowd and someone was afraid."

"I—I was making up a story. I'm going to write books when I'm older."

Mrs. Barstow smiled at Lyd, brilliantly. She suddenly looked much younger and almost pretty. Before that Lyd had thought her face interesting and alive, but certainly not pretty.

"You could," said Mrs. Barstow. "I wanted to write books myself, but I turned to painting instead. What happened, Lyd Allbright?"

Lyd said, without thinking, "I'm not really Lyd Allbright. I'm Cornish."

"You mean you were adopted? It's obvious you're different from the rest of the family."

"Did someone tell you? My father wouldn't."

"Oh, no. But you look so different. A real little Celt. I couldn't help wondering about it."

"I don't think I want to be here!" Lyd burst out, driven into sudden speech. "I thought I could face it, but now I'm not sure I can. I want to go back to Bristol and not know about it. She was happy in her garden, and the cat was happy, too."

Mrs. Barstow said nothing. Lyd stared at her, then around the living room of the cottage, which was bathed in late afternoon light. Then she began to tell about some of the things that had happened, saying she couldn't tell her family, because they'd be angry or upset and would think she was making it up. At first, she said, the thing had been just in that part of the lane where the cottage was, but this time it had been right down the lane, there by the honeysuckle—nothing really seen, but a feeling that there was a crowd and someone terribly scared.

"Do you believe in ghosts?" asked Lyd desperately at the end.

"No," said Mrs. Barstow calmly. "Not actually in ghosts, that is, people who have come back from another world. I don't believe in another world."

"After people are dead, you mean?" Lyd's interest was caught. "Not in heaven or hell, or any of those things? I thought everyone believed something. I thought . . . well, that one had to."

Mrs. Barstow laughed, and Lyd went pink. That had been a childish remark, unworthy of a supposedly clever girl who was maybe going to study to go to college.

"I mean, I know there are agnostics and atheists, or people who say they are. We have a girl at school who says her father's a humanist. And my parents aren't *religious,* but we go to church sometimes. Tom and Jeff and I were always sent to Sunday school. I've sometimes felt wicked because it was rather difficult to . . . well, to believe. But I did think one had to pretend to."

"There's no law about it, Lyd," her new friend said. "Someday you'll decide for yourself what you believe or don't believe, and you'll work out some kind of philosophy. I don't believe myself that people exist in any way after death, so I can't believe in ghosts, can I? But I *can* just believe in something hanging in the air of a certain place. Forever, perhaps. And maybe someone especially sensitive can become aware of it. Did you ever hear anything? Smell anything?

Lyd thought. She was soothed to be treated in this calm, reasonable way.

"No. There was a lavender bush, but I couldn't smell it, and I think rosemary—we have a bush in our little garden at home. But of course I wasn't very near, in any case. And I never heard anything. Just saw and—and felt that awful feeling of cold fear."

"Mainly a picture hanging in the air," said Mrs. Barstow, almost to herself. "Do you know anything about Trelonyan, Lyd?"

"Its history, you mean? No, I don't. I read one book

about Cornwall, but it didn't say anything. But something happened here, and I—I think I have to see it all. I'm scared; I don't want to. But I think I will."

"Can't you tell your father and mother? They ought to know how you feel."

"No, I can't and I won't. They'd laugh or be angry. Saul said I should tell them."

"Saul knows?"

"Yes, I didn't explain that. He was with me on two of the occasions. I didn't mean to tell *anyone*. Do you—do you believe me?" Lyd felt that the answer would be very important.

Mrs. Barstow hesitated. After a short while she said, "I've never felt or experienced anything like that myself, and I've never before met anyone who claimed that he had. I find life on the whole cold and practical, yet I *have* felt this to be a strange place. I believe you really think you have seen something."

"I did. I saw and felt. I didn't smell and I couldn't touch. I tried to touch the cat, but he was only a gauzy shadow, though his fur shone so healthily and he *looked* real." She ate another cookie.

"I think that you should go away," said Mrs. Barstow, after a long silence.

Lyd froze, staring at her. "Home to Bristol? Before the vacation is over?"

"Well, if I were your parents, I'd take you away. You said you wanted to go."

"But—but this is their holiday, and they're loving every minute of it, and in a way I like it, too. I—I like Saul, and we're friends. No, I couldn't tell them, not only because they wouldn't believe me, but because I really wouldn't want to spoil it for them all. Besides, I'm not a baby; I'm sixteen. In a strange way I feel much older than I did a few days ago. It was just that it was so unexpected this afternoon. *You* won't tell them?" Lyd asked, in fright.

"Of course not; you told me in confidence. But I don't think this is quite the place for you. It's a mystery why it should happen to you, even though you're Cornish."

"Yes, it is strange. Well, I didn't have a Cornish name, but I think I was born near Bodmin." Lyd scrambled to her feet in a sudden hurry to be gone. "Thank you *very* much for the tea, and for listening." She paused, standing very straight and suddenly sounding very sure of herself. "I don't believe it's *me*. They won't harm me. They're only shadows, so they can't. I think you're right. It's something that happened in the past and it's still here. I'm not half as scared as I was at first, though I know it was something terrible. It's a mystery, but I think I'll know the answer before it's over. I'm going now. Good-bye." And she went away, walking very quickly down the flower-edged path.

Mrs. Barstow slowly removed the things from the table and, as she worked, her brow was creased by a puzzled frown. It *was* a mystery. Her mind was filled with thoughts of the girl who had just gone, and that, she told herself wryly, was better than feeling sorry for herself because just lately life had treated her so badly. Lyd Allbright . . . strange little dark-haired thing. She expressed herself well and clearly once she really started talking, and it was certain that she sincerely believed there was something unusual about Trelonyan Cove. Of course it could all be some kind of illusion, or a lively imagination getting out of hand.

If she had heard the story from someone else and not seen the girl pressed against the bank in shrinking fear, Mrs. Barstow would have dismissed it with a laugh. No, maybe not with a laugh, but she wouldn't have believed it. She did pretty well believe Lyd, but she could understand that the other members of her family wouldn't be able to swallow the tale. Only, if they thought the place bad for Lyd for whatever reason, wouldn't they take her away?

Yet, as Lyd had said, she wasn't a baby. Mrs. Barstow had the definite feeling that she had been facing a rapidly developing human being. And that was good . . . to face up to things and surmount fear. But whatever it was that had taken place in Trelonyan Cove and its environs might well be too much for a sensitive sixteen-year-old girl who, Mrs. Barstow felt without any knowledge, had always found life difficult.

CHAPTER SEVEN

The Lost Manor House

After supper Lyd walked to the Cove. Deliberately and very slowly, she went by the longer route, the broad path that ended near the Trelonyan Arms. The evening was hot and very still. As she started downward she could look up almost the whole length of the brooding valley, where the close-growing trees were quite motionless and of such a dark green that, in the already gathering shadows, they looked almost black.

The sky was still blue and the sun was shining, but the light only touched the tops of the trees near the head of the deep incline and the high, harsh cliff to her right. Voices and laughter rose on the quiet air, and when she leaned on the bank to look down, she could see people sitting at the tables outside the Trelonyan Arms.

She felt curiously relaxed and tired, but not in any way unhappy. In retrospect the long conversation with Mrs. Barstow and her comments about religion and finding one's own philosophy made good thinking. Until then Lyd had shunned too much thought on the subject, but the idea that she might work things out for herself sud-

denly seemed to her splendid. It was another opening
door. Also she really thought that Mrs. Barstow had believed her strange story, and that had been a help.

So, slowly, stopping to look at the little life of the high
banks, Lyd came down onto the road. Equally slowly she
walked over to where the honeysuckle grew and picked
a few sweet-smelling blossoms. Nothing at all happened;
the place remained calm and untroubled. She was evi-
dently not on that wave length now.

She turned and strolled past the inn, and Mrs. Clark,
coming out with a tray laden with glasses of beer and
lemonade, smiled warmly at her. Lyd waved back and
went on, stopping once more to test the big red blackberries. One or two were turning black, but they weren't
going to be ripe until long after the Allbrights had left
Trelonyan Cove.

Down by the Cove the boats seemed to be in, and only
one car was parked there. Three people were standing
at the far end of the quay, near the old beacon. Otherwise,
the place was deserted, and the shadows already lay across
the empty cottages.

Lyd was leaning on the harbor wall when Saul came
back from Penzance. He knew at once that something had
happened, though Lyd tried to hide it at first.

"I went to have tea with Mrs. Barstow," she said
quickly. "She gave me muffins and chocolate cookies and
we talked. She's nice, Saul."

"Yes, she is," Saul agreed. "So why are you looking like
that, Lyd—full of secrets? Did something happen while
I was away?"

Lyd leaned her back against the wall, which was still
warm from the day's hot sun, and stared at him. The
bright evening light fell on his dark face, and her heart
seemed to contract with a sudden dull pain. Briefly and

strangely, she thought: Am I in love with him? Could I
be? And, if so, what shall I do? Because Bristol is a long
way from here. Can I really be in love at sixteen?

Suddenly Saul was far more important than the mystery, so she was startled when he said, without waiting
for an answer, "I think you should go away from here."

"But why, Saul? Mrs. Barstow said that too. I couldn't,
anyway. How could I spoil their vacation? I'm all right,
really. I'm not hurt. I'm—I'm used to it, and I don't think
I can escape."

Saul had the story out of her in a few minutes. He
seemed deeply troubled, perhaps even more upset than
seemed wholly reasonable.

"I don't like it," he said forcefully. "Can't you *try* to
tell your parents? Give them the opportunity of deciding
whether you should stay here or not?"

"No, I can't." Lyd was suddenly angry and miserable.
One of the things she minded most about the whole
strange affair was that it was putting an invisible barrier
between her and her family. But she really felt that this
was something she had to face up to and deal with almost
alone. Did Saul *want* her to go away? Wouldn't he miss
her? The thought that he might forget her as soon as she
was gone was a sharp, added pain of a kind that was quite
new to her.

"All right. Keep your hair on." He was suddenly more
schoolboy than grown-up young man. "I won't force you
to do anything. You know that. I couldn't, anyway. You
may be little, but you have character."

"Have I, Saul?" Lyd cheered up.

"You certainly have. Didn't you know?"

"No-o, I didn't. Sometimes I've felt as if I only half
existed. But just lately I've felt different."

"Well, I must go home now, but I'll take an hour or two

off in the morning. There's something I want to show you, Lyd. Will you meet me here at ten o'clock?"

"Oh, yes." She hoped she hadn't sounded too eager. She said good-bye and quickly went back up the narrow path to the cottage. Collie met her halfway up, barking and pleased to see her. Light was already streaming through the cottage windows. She saw her parents and Tom and Jeff in the living room.

What a strange day it had been . . . well, since late afternoon. Life was puzzling and worrying, but more interesting than she had ever imagined. Dreams were no good now, not the kind of dreams she had indulged in until recently. She was up against something real—two things real: her growing feeling for Saul and the mystery of Trelonyan Cove.

But, wondered Lyd, as she entered the cottage, can I call the mystery "real"? It seems real to me, and there must have been a reality sometime—that's what I'm scared of. But whatever it was, it must have been over and done with long ago.

When Lyd met Saul the next morning, he said, "We're going to climb up the cliff over there. Not where it's dangerous. The way I'll take you, it's just a stiff scramble. It's rather nice on top on that side, and you haven't been there yet. One can see for miles."

Lyd stared up at the uninviting cliff and at the equally harsh hillside running inland, and at first she wasn't keen, but once they had started climbing, she began to enjoy herself. There were rocks and loose stones and here and there gorse bushes and stunted trees. There was also a faint suggestion of a path, although sometimes it disappeared and Saul had to put out his hand to haul her up after him. His fingers were warm and pleasant to hold.

Hard physical exercise was what Lyd needed just then, and she felt a real sense of triumph and achievement as she reached the top. The harbor lay immediately below, and on the opposite cliff, just visible behind bushes and low trees, was Mrs. Barstow's cottage. The sea was dazzling blue, as it had been almost every day of her visit.

When she swung around to gaze east she could indeed see for miles, even as far as the outjutting Lizard Peninsula.

A hundred yards or so away, across the rough, stony land, was a big green hollow, and Saul led her toward it. The shallow valley was edged with gorse, but down below, all overgrown, was what looked like the ruins of a house. Here and there part of a stone wall stood up, and in the tallest piece there were still traces of a mullioned window.

"Oh!" Lyd gazed in wonder at the abandoned place. "Is this why you brought me up here? What was it like? When did it go? Who lived here?"

"It was Trelonyan Manor," Saul explained. "The Trelonyan family lived here. For a long, long time it was empty, and then it fell down. I suppose people took away the stones for other buildings. That's what usually happens. People always need building stone."

"But how do you know who lived here?"

"Mrs. Barstow told me. I met her up here one day. She was curious about the place. There's a very old man living in St. Buryan who's something of an authority on the archaeology of Cornwall. He was sitting in his garden one day and they got talking. He told her the family fortunes gradually declined, and the last people were very poor and did nothing to the house. Then the family died out and the place has been empty for the last hundred years."

"A hundred years," Lyd repeated. "I wish I knew what

it used to look like. I wonder how they got up here?
There's no road."

"There are traces of one from that far end of the hollow. It heads toward the main road, then just disappears.
It may have been a real road once." After a pause Saul
asked, "Want to go down there? It's terribly brambly,
but the middle of the house is all right."

"Yes, let's go," Lyd agreed. "But it looks like an awfully
sad place."

"It doesn't give you the cold feeling? You can't *see* what
it used to look like?" Saul's voice was half mocking, half
curious.

"No. Nothing. It's just sad. How awful to live there
with no money to keep the house beautiful. I like the
shape of that window, the curve of the stone tracery. And
then there was no one left?"

"It may have been just as well," Saul remarked, as he
led the way down into the hollow. The golden gorse
smelled nutty and sweet in the hot sun, and brambles
tore at Lyd's bare legs. The ground was uneven, with long
grass here and there, but soon they were in the shallow
bowl, with everything shut out but the arching, dark-
blue sky.

"You can see where the foundations were all the way
around," Saul explained. "But except for these bits of
walls, there really isn't anything left."

Bees and other insects made a loud humming noise,
and it wasn't really sad in the middle of what had once
been a big house. There were small trees casting patches
of shade, and Saul flung himself on the grass. Lyd sat
beside him, looking down at his long, slender body. It was
strange to be in this secret place, but she was happy,
forgetting the ghostly emanations on the road to Trelonyan Cove.

She thought, almost sleepily, about the house that had once stood where they were. People had been born here, had lived out their lives, and died. There must have been big rooms, sunlit on summer days such as this, and maybe shrouded in gloom when mist lay over the sea. If she really had any power to see the past, she almost wished it might be extended to include this lost house.

"What are you thinking?" asked Saul, squinting up at her against the brilliant light.

"About the house. Wondering why I can't see it, when I can see that cottage." Lyd, relaxed, spoke quite naturally. "Do you know, Saul, I almost wish I could. One could learn so much."

"Don't you try," Saul retorted. "Let it rest, or sleep, or whatever it's doing. That's the best thing for anything in the past."

"But the past leads to the present, doesn't it? Things never quite finish. Perhaps there's . . . a continuing line."

"Not here. The family died out."

Quite a long time later Saul sat up and said he ought to go back and help with the boats. Anyway, it would soon be lunch time. Suddenly, totally unexpectedly, he leaned sideways and kissed Lyd on the mouth. Lyd gasped and stared at him, and he laughed.

"Hasn't anyone ever kissed you before, Lyd?" he asked.

"Oh, yes, once or twice. At parties, you know. But I don't like parties much, and the kisses didn't mean anything."

"That one did," Saul said gravely. "You grow prettier every day, Lyd, in spite of these strange things that have been happening to you."

Warmth filled Lyd's heart, and she was conscious that a little stab of awareness and joy had gone through her whole body at the moment of the kiss. She felt that she had grown up several months in a few seconds. If only she didn't have the mystery hanging over her, and that awful feeling that she was cut off from her family, she would have been happier than ever before in her life.

"So you don't want me to go away?" she asked, and at once Saul was grave in a different way.

"I don't want it, but I think you maybe should. Look here, Lyd, we're friends, aren't we?"

"Oh, *yes.*"

"Well, I have the most definite feeling that we'll meet again. I told you, I may be going to Bristol University. And there's another thing. I have an uncle, my father's brother, who is a long-distance truck driver. He works for a firm in Redruth, and he sometimes goes through Bristol. I could cadge a lift and come to see you. It would be dead easy."

That was wonderful, but still she couldn't go away now. It was impossible. As they slithered down the side of the cliff Saul didn't argue the point, but went on to tell her that he also had an aunt, his mother's sister, who was a widow and lived near Hugh Town on St. Mary's, the largest of the Scilly Isles. She had been ill, and his mother wanted him to go over for a day and see her.

"We're going into Penzance tomorrow," Lyd remarked. "I wish I could go to the Scilly Isles too. I've only once been on an island, and that was Lundy."

Saul made no answer to that, though she was afraid she had been fishing for an invitation. Perhaps he didn't want to say anything that would encourage her to stay.

As they reached the flat, rough land behind Saul's cottage, Lyd said suddenly, "That old man who lives in St. Buryan, Saul. Do you think he'd know about the Cove? I mean, whether anything important ever happened here, and whether there *was* a cottage in the wood—that is, where the wood is now?"

"I shouldn't think so," Saul said quickly. "He's interested mainly in archaeology: standing stones and burial mounds and things. And he isn't a local man. Mrs. Barstow said he used to live in Truro and only came to St. Buryan a few years ago. Besides, he's about ninety and very feeble. She said his housekeeper hovered around him like an anxious hen."

Probably Saul was right and it wouldn't be a good thing to go and see the old man, but for a moment Lyd felt vaguely dissatisfied. Then, as she ran over the little stone bridge, the feeling disappeared and she only remembered Saul's warm kiss and his remark that she was pretty. She felt she would always cherish the memory of the lost manor house and the sunny green hollow where they had sat under the trees.

Lyd saw suddenly that Tom and Jeff were walking along the quay, so she waited for them at the bottom of the path that led up to Tamarisk Cottage.

She had not realized that her face was so telltale, but Tom asked at once, "Gosh, Lyd, have you come into a fortune?"

"No. Why?"

"I don't know. You look kind of glowing. We saw you climbing down the cliff with Saul. Where have you been?"

"To see a lost manor house," Lyd explained, thankfully going ahead of them up the narrow path. "It's up there, in a hollow . . . just walls and one window. You should go and look."

But lost manor houses were not one of the boys' interests, and they dismissed the matter as just some place that romantic Lyd found fascinating.

Before they reached the cottage Lyd thought she had

composed her face, and that her joy really was secret, but her mother, like Tom, glanced at her quickly. "I must say you look well, Lyd," she said. "Did you have a good morning?"

"Finding a lost manor house or something," said Jeff.

"That sounds right up Lyd's alley. Where is it?"

"On the other cliff," Lyd mumbled, and went to wash her hands. It wasn't so much the lost manor that had altered her appearance, though it still filled her imagination, but that little kiss, so unexpectedly given. She felt curiously exposed, and she wondered why it was so hard to hide her emotions. Was it a thing one learned with advancing years? Maybe at twenty she would be really inscrutable. But twenty seemed such a great age that she could hardly believe she would ever reach it.

Mrs. Allbright said no more, but she suspected, as Tom and Jeff did not, that the relationship with Saul was growing. And, if it made Lyd look like that, it could only be a good thing, surely. She had sensed at times that something was wrong, but today everything seemed fine and that was a relief.

Lyd went down to help Saul in the afternoon, and they worked so hard that they had no time for talking. He didn't suggest again that she go away, and the kiss might have been a dream, for he seemed no more than a good friend with whom she was at ease.

At dusk Lyd leaned on the bank and gazed down at the Cove, already deep in shadow. Go away? Well, they all would when the two weeks were over. What a comfort it was to remember that Saul might come to see her in Bristol.

She did not write about the kiss in her diary, when, later, she sat on her bed and scribbled in the precious book. Generally she wrote down everything important that happened as well as random thoughts, but the kiss was something she did not want to put into words.

I wish I knew more about Trelonyan Manor [she wrote], although I'm not sure that I want to know about the mystery. Still, if I don't learn what happened to the old woman and the cat, I shall never be quite satisfied, even though I know it must have been something terrible.

Oh, I was happy today! Happy in the green hollow. And again this afternoon, helping Saul with the boats. If life were all like that, how wonderful it would be.

CHAPTER EIGHT

An Island Interlude

Early the next day the Allbrights went into Penzance, and Lyd asked if they could go and watch the Scilly Isles steamer leave. The *Scillonian* was a small ship, but the dock workers made a lot of bustle loading crates and boxes as well as some farm machinery. A good many tourists were also going out to the remote islands, and Lyd watched them enviously. It would be wonderful to go to St. Mary's, or to Tresco with its famous gardens, or to Samson, or to others that were hardly more than uninhabited rocks.

"Saul says he may be going over to Hugh Town for the day," she remarked. "He has an aunt who lives there."

"You go with him if you want," said her father. "The day excursion fare isn't very high, and it would be an interesting experience for you. However, I hear this is one of the worst crossings around Britain. When the ship sails around Land's End it hits a lot of currents."

Lyd was silent, because Saul had not invited her to accompany him. For a moment her heart contracted, and part of her wished violently that she were still in Trelonyan, helping him with the boats. All the same, it was interesting to explore the narrow old streets of Penzance, and to see the palm trees and semitropical plants in the Morrab Gardens.

During their wanderings she saw the Public Library and stopped. "Have I time to go in here and look up some Cornish books? They must have plenty in the reference room."

But Tom and Jeff set up such a loud complaint that she was forced to give up the idea. They had a picnic lunch with them, as well as swimming things, and the plan was to go to Marazion, just a short distance along the coast.

When they arrived there, Lyd was thrilled, for it was a romantic place. The little town stretched above the rocky shore, and as the tide was out, the stone causeway to St. Michael's Mount was visible all the way to the island. The Mount rose up against the blue sky, crowned by the castle.

They ate quickly, then set off across the causeway, walking barefoot over the slippery stones, while a soft, warm breeze blew around them. On the island a few stone cottages nestled at the foot of the crag, and a path wound up and up to the high castle. It was one of those days when the chapel and some of the rooms were open to the public, and Lyd found everything fascinating. She tried to imagine what it would be like to live in such a place; it was a far cry from their ordinary little house in Bristol.

They returned in a small boat, because the tide had covered the causeway, and then they all undressed behind high rocks and swam. Later Tom and Jeff played ball on a stretch of sand that the tide had not reached, while Mr. and Mrs. Allbright settled themselves against some rocks and read newspapers. Lyd lay stretched out on the sand for a time, then unaccountably became restless. The sky was blue, the sun was hot, and she had thought she felt lazy, but suddenly it was as if something were drawing her away.

She sat up. Her father's paper had dropped down and he was asleep; her mother was also nodding. Tom and Jeff, some distance away, were absorbed in their game and paying no attention to her. Lyd rose and walked slowly but purposefully toward the steps cut in the rock. She walked up the narrow lane, then along the main road for some distance, and finally down another lane that led toward the sea again. She felt bemused and hardly knew what she was doing.

The lane was short and no one was in sight. The dazzling light of afternoon struck back from a white wall, and there were pink and scarlet trails of small roses. Then there was nothing but gray stone walls, ending on the rocks above the sea. The stone walls formed a low square, thickly overgrown inside with nettles and wild flowers.

Lyd sat on the piece of wall nearest the lane. She did not feel cold as she usually did; rather she felt pleasantly hot, as the sun touched her bare arms and legs. St. Michael's Mount seemed to float on the water, and the only sounds were the wash of the waves below and the cries of gulls. But she was suddenly fully aware of the fact that she felt strange. Why had she come here? It was almost as if someone had brought her, or as if some force had directed her footsteps.

The wall on which she sat, no more than two feet high, had probably once been part of a cottage. Was she haunted by cottages? She gazed all around, yet there was nothing but sunny peace and the faint, elusive sense of something just out of reach. The feeling was not frightening, but compelling. What possible connection could this ruined cottage—this almost vanished cottage—have with Trelonyan? It was impossible to know, but she was convinced that there was some joining thread. Mere chance had not brought her here.

Her mother found her still sitting there a short time later. "Oh, there you are, Lyd!" she cried. "I saw you go and thought I'd like a walk. I hate sleeping in the daytime. Why, what's the matter?"

"Nothing, Mother. Nothing." The strange feelings had fled; Lyd was herself again.

"I thought . . . you looked far away as I came down the lane. I suppose this must have been a cottage once. What a lovely place to live, with this wonderful view."

"Yes. But we don't know who lived here."

"Lyd . . ." Mrs. Allbright began, but at that moment they heard shouts down below and saw Tom and Jeff, who had walked along the beach and over the rocks toward them.

"You can get down quite easily," Jeff called.

But it wasn't easy, at least not for Mrs. Allbright, but she and Lyd found what path there was and presently reached the beach. Afterward Lyd thought that she might have brought herself to tell her mother about the moments of possession if Tom and Jeff hadn't suddenly appeared. She didn't know whether to be glad or sorry that they had been interrupted.

Going down the Trelonyan lane in the late afternoon, she again saw the cottage in the wood dimly. Once past it, Lyd thought again of the library. There must be a way to find out if something had ever happened in Trelonyan Cove. Almost everything was in books.

Mr. Allbright had suggested driving to Falmouth the next day, saying that they really must see more of Cornwall instead of fishing all the time. Lyd saw no way of escaping, but was cheered to spend an hour or two with Saul after supper. They strolled on the quay and then went to his home, where he played some of his records for her. One of his few possessions was a cheap record player, which had been given him, he said, by his uncle on his seventeenth birthday.

Mr. and Mrs. Treporth were sitting outside the cottage in the warm evening, so Lyd and Saul had the living room to themselves. Some of the records were orchestral ones, mainly by modern composers like Malcolm Arnold, but there were some "pop" records, too. Suddenly Saul laughed and began to dance in the restricted space, and Lyd jumped up and moved with him to the exciting beat. Now one of her early questions was answered: Saul could dance.

Before she left, Lyd explained about going to Falmouth the next day, and was a little hurt because Saul didn't seem to mind. The time was slipping away so rapidly that she felt she wanted to be with him as much as possible. But she couldn't hurt her family, either.

Saul walked with her to the bottom of the path, and after she had left him, she remembered that she had not told him about that strange little episode in Marazion. Maybe it was just as well. She didn't want to say anything that would remind him of the effect certain things could have on her. She was *not* going to leave until she had to.

Lyd's resolution had been to spend another day with her family, but the next day, as they were driving through Penzance toward Falmouth, she suddenly spoke almost without thought.

"Look!" she said. "Would you mind if I didn't go with you? I have something I want to do here."

She was sitting in front with her father, and he glanced

at her curiously. "What is it, Lyd? What's so interesting?"

"I want to go and read up on Cornwall in the library, Dad. I really want to learn more, and I may not have another chance."

Mr. Allbright was impressed. He might say hard things about students, but in his secret heart he valued learning and the desire to learn. This adopted daughter of his was clever. If she wanted to add to her knowledge, who was he to hold her back?

Tom and Jeff jeered. "Oh, come on, Lyd! Stuffing indoors on such a day!"

Mrs. Allbright was not quite happy. "But don't you want to see Falmouth, Lyd?" she asked. "And what will you do later?"

"I'll have a sandwich somewhere and walk part of the way back. You don't mind, do you, Mother?"

Mrs. Allbright did mind, but knew she was being unreasonable. By then they were almost out of the town, and when the car stopped, Lyd slid out quickly. As she turned back toward Market Jew Street, she felt guilty and rather dishonest. It wasn't general knowledge of Cornwall she wanted, but information about Trelonyan Cove, where something unusual must have happened once.

Market Jew Street was crowded and busy and very hot. Lyd climbed the steep hill, panting a little. After a few minutes she realized with surprise that it was good to be free, and that made her feel more guilty than ever. How mixed up she was, wanting to be close to her family, and longing at the same time to escape.

Anyway, here she was in Penzance, and in a few minutes more she reached the library. Indoors it was darkish and seemed cool after the heat of the sun. She stopped to look at some notices, then turned to the reference room. She was just putting in her request for any books that mentioned Trelonyan Cove when she felt a hand on her arm.

"Hi, Lyd!" said Saul. "I saw you come in and hurried after you." He was carrying the two plastic shopping bags, already fairly full, and sounded breathless.

Lyd hesitated, torn between joy and irritation, but before she could speak, Saul went on. "Do come with me. I'm going to have coffee with a school friend—a nice chap. You'll like him."

"But—but I was going to read some Cornish books."

"Oh, you can do that anytime."

Somehow Saul had steered her out of the library and headed her back to Market Jew Street. Lyd went willingly enough, for it was hard to resist his company, but a little feeling of frustration remained.

"Saul, I do want to see if any books say something about Trelonyan and find out whether anything special ever happened there, you know."

"I've looked," he said. "There isn't anything."

"When?"

"Oh, last time I was in town." Saul's voice was a trifle hurried, but Lyd didn't notice at the time.

"You didn't tell me."

"No, because there was nothing to tell. I thought you were going to Falmouth today."

"Yes, I was, but just as the car was leaving Penzance, I changed my mind. Where are you meeting your friend?"

"Here." Saul opened the door of a coffee shop.

The friend was waiting, a handsome boy of eighteen called John Polgarth. He seemed to admire Lyd, and she didn't feel as shy as usual. The conversation was interesting, too, for she learned something about the school they had both now left, and, as she had never before seen Saul with a contemporary, she felt she had learned more about him.

Presently, after doing some more shopping, she and Saul took the bus back to the signpost at the top of the lane, and Saul invited her to have lunch with his family.

"Of course you must come," he said. "You don't want to go back to your cottage alone. There's plenty of *fish.*" And they both laughed, because fish did seem to be the staple diet.

They returned by the footpath, and neither of them mentioned the "cold place" at all. The Treporths did not seem surprised by Lyd's arrival, and she found that she now felt quite at ease with them.

"It's good for them to have company," said Saul, as they went down to the Cove later. "It makes my father much brighter and helps him to forget the pain."

They were busy most of the afternoon, but during a pause Saul said, "I'm going over to St. Mary's tomorrow. How'd you like to come with me? Mr. Pendennis is going into Penzance in time for the steamer and will give us a lift."

Lyd was enchanted. Go with Saul to those far islands! Her slight frustration over the library was forgotten, and even the importance of the mystery seemed diminished.

"But be warned," Saul went on. "It can be an awful crossing. You heard the forecast: the weather will be fine and hot for another two or three days, but with a chance of wind and occasional thunderstorms."

"I wasn't sick going to Lundy," said Lyd. "I'll risk it."

So the next morning there they were on the quay. Saul carried a parcel for his aunt, containing a sweater his mother had knitted, and Lyd walked easily, with her red shoulder bag swinging slightly. The morning was warm, but without a doubt it was windier. Even in Mount's Bay there were waves. Saul looked at the water and laughed. "Don't blame me!"

Lyd thought how ignominious it would be to be seasick in front of Saul, but hoped for the best. Although the crossing would take only two or three hours, she was as excited as if she were setting off for America.

They would be there in good time for lunch.

Saul had said his aunt was looking forward to having an extra visitor; she had a telephone, and he had spoken to her from the booth outside the post office the previous evening.

The little ship was very crowded, but Saul found them good places on a kind of bulwark under a slight overhang.

"We may want to hang on if it's rough," he said. "If you sit out there on the seats, you can be drenched with spray. And it can be awful down below. You don't want to be indoors, do you?"

Lyd didn't. She was delighted to be able to see all she could, even the heaving blue sea as they left Mount's Bay and headed west. But after they had left Land's End behind, the water grew very rough, and a good many people succumbed to the unpleasant conditions.

Lyd, happy and relaxed, was relieved to find that she still felt perfectly well, and was even exhilarated by the light of the sky and the brilliantly blue sea. But the little ship was swaying too much for walking around. She and Saul clung to their not very comfortable perch and talked.

On and on they went, across what seemed like a vast ocean. Ahead lay the islands, but she could not see them yet. The bow dipped and rose; spray swept overboard in great white clouds. Some of the less happy tourists screamed and then looked ashamed.

And I'm not scared, Lyd thought in wonder. I *must*

have changed. Only a short time ago I'd have been sure
we were going to the bottom with each wave. Maybe I'd
be scared if Saul weren't with me.

Sometimes Saul put his arm around her and held her
securely as the ship went down into the trough of a wave.
Lyd leaned her head against his shoulder, and remained
contented in a heaving world. And then the islands were
ahead of them. At first they only saw wild headlands and
deserted beaches, but at last, an hour later, they turned
into a wide, quiet bay, where white houses stood on the
hillsides and a little gray town lay around a harbor. Hugh
Town, St. Mary's. It was like a dream, this arrival in still
waters in a blaze of light and warmth after the hours on
the rough sea.

They walked along the main street. Most of the buildings were of granite and not pretty. There was a grim air
about the town, but it was mitigated by the sunlight and
the blue sky. The wind had dropped and it was really
warm.

"It seems strange," mused Lyd, "that people live here
all the time, that it's still Britain, though so remote. And
traffic! I never expected cars and trucks and buses."

Saul laughed. "You ought to see more; you ought to go
to Tresco and St. Martin's. But there isn't time. Maybe
you'll come back one day."

His aunt, Mrs. Pendene, lived in a small bungalow on
a hill above Hugh Town. From the road outside the gate
they could see for miles, to some of the other islands
and over the two bays on which Hugh Town stood. Mrs.
Pendene was a small, dark-haired woman, who looked
pale and not very well, but she was animated and had
plenty to say. She embarrased Lyd by asking:

"Is this your girl friend, Saul? Well, she's pretty, or she

will be when she fills out. Are you Cornish, my dear?"

Lyd, blushing, confessed that she might be, and Mrs. Pendene didn't seem curious about her after that. Saul didn't seem embarrassed at all.

At lunch Lyd ate well, and felt as if she were a thousand miles from Britain on this remote island. They sat and drank their coffee in a little garden bowered with roses, and Saul gave all the family news and asked for news in return. Lyd listened, and sometimes dreamed, and played with a white cat. Time passed so quickly that she was surprised when Saul rose and said they must return to the quay.

They still had time to stroll in quite a leisurely way along the main street. Lyd looked in the windows of the little stores and bought some postcards. She felt, quite definitely, that the day had been an interlude between more important affairs, but it was a wonderful interlude, even with another wild crossing so soon in store.

However, the crossing back to Penzance wasn't wild. The sea had grown much calmer and the little ship went steadily on its way. As Land's End came into view and the sea turned more green than blue, a party of young men began to sing. They were members of a rowing club from Newquay, and they sang in harmony, so beautifully that Lyd gradually sank into an enchanted dream.

They sat, for the most part, in the same place as before, and she leaned against Saul, very much aware of him, but at the same time carried away by the rising voices and the evening light on the calm sea. Then, as the high cliffs of the Land's End Peninsula came in view, they stood by the rail and stared at the passing scene: Porthcurno, then Trelonyan Cove, its deep valley dark and secret looking as it came down to the water.

Suddenly Lyd turned and surprised a strange expression on Saul's face. He was gazing at his home with a look she could not read.

"It looks eerie even from this distance," she said. "Oh, Saul, it is an odd place! Those empty cottages and lofts . . . I can't see them, not properly, but I can see the trees and the cliffs. The manor is up there. . . . Saul, I have to know more."

"No!" he said, so sharply that she jumped.

"Why not?"

"It's better not to find out. Go away and forget it."

They were past Trelonyan already. There was Lamorna and then they were turning into Mount's Bay. Suddenly, uneasily, Lyd began to wonder. She remembered how quickly Saul had taken her away from the library, where she might have learned about Trelonyan Cove. She remembered how he had never seemed to want her to pursue the mystery of her strange experiences, and how he had said she ought to go away on more than one occasion. She had simply thought that he believed the place bad for her, but now she asked herself if Saul knew more than he had admitted. If he did, that meant there was some truth somewhere in what she had seen and felt. It could not be a figment of her imagination.

Saul didn't even belong to Trelonyan Cove, but Newlyn was not very far from it. She looked at him again, but his dark face was inscrutable and he seemed to have gone away from her. Sadly, aware that the happiness of the day was somehow spoiled, she knew that she dared not say any more, or ask any questions.

The young men were softly singing *Good Night, Ladies* as the ship moved toward the quay at Penzance. The water was almost apple-green in the brilliant evening light,

and the town climbed the hill, crowned by the great land-
mark of the church.

They ran for the bus and were mainly silent as it passed
through Newlyn and then struggled up the steep slope
to the bleak, bare country beyond. When they left the
bus at the signpost, they saw Mr. Allbright waiting in
the car.

"I thought you'd catch this bus," he said. "Did you have
a good day?"

He drove them down the lane, unimpeded by traffic.
The cottage was there again, a shadow in the shadowy
wood. Lyd saw it with only a slight chill, for her mind
was busy. The day *had* been good, and it was a pity it
had to end with tension between her and Saul. Probably
she was wrong and he knew nothing, because, if he had
knowledge, she could think of no valid reason why he
should want to keep it from her.

CHAPTER NINE

The Thunderstorm

Lyd spent a disturbed night, sometimes dwelling on the happy events of the previous day, but occasionally waking to worry about Saul. He *had* looked and sounded strange—there was no doubt about that—she had not questioned him beyond that startled "Why not?" She had not done anything that could have annoyed him, so it was silly to feel troubled and vaguely guilty.

During breakfast her mother glanced at her once or twice, and Lyd noted the fact uneasily. Her wretched face always seemed to give things away. But all her mother asked was, "I suppose you'll be helping Saul again today?"

Lyd said yes, she supposed she would, and hoped she was right. She walked slowly down the path to the Cove, and met Mrs. Barstow near the bottom. Since that afternoon when they had had tea together, Lyd had seen her once or twice to speak to briefly.

Mrs. Barstow was still painting near Porthcurno, and she was just about to mount her bicycle and ride away. However, she stopped when she saw Lyd. "How are you,

101

Lyd?" she asked. "I heard you went to St. Mary's with Saul."

"Yes. It was wonderful." Lyd paused, then burst out, "Mrs. Barstow, do you think Saul knows anything about the history of Trelonyan Cove?"

Mrs. Barstow didn't look surprised. She leaned on her bicycle and surveyed Lyd. "I don't know. He only came to live here a year or two ago. Why do you ask?"

"Please don't tell him I asked. It's just a feeling I had yesterday evening. As we sailed past Trelonyan in the evening he looked so strange and spoke so sharply. I—I suddenly felt he did believe me over the things that have happened, and—and had some knowledge. I didn't really notice at the time, but later . . . What could he know?"

Mrs. Barstow shook her head. "I really have no idea. Has anything more happened, Lyd?"

It was a relief to talk, and Lyd no longer felt shy with Mrs. Barstow. She told about the strange little episode in Marazion, and how the cottage in the wood was still there.

"Marazion. . . . That's odd!" said Mrs. Barstow. Lyd was relieved that she seemed merely interested and didn't seem to be intending to say again that Lyd should go away. "But you didn't see anything?"

"Nothing. Just felt as if I were drawn there. I didn't tell Saul that. I could so easily have imagined it, couldn't I?"

"You could," said her companion. "Look, there's Saul waving to you. I expect he needs your help. People are arriving already."

Lyd nodded and ran to join Saul. To her vast relief he seemed just as usual and greeted her warmly. They spent a busy and happy morning, and Lyd returned to the cottage at twelve-thirty glowing and cheerful.

After the meal her mother said, "Lyd, will you run

down to the post office for me? I want some stamps and a few other things. Here's a list and the money."

Lyd took a shopping bag and slowly set off down the path. It was very hot, though not as sunny as usual. The air was heavy, and she thought uneasily that it was going to thunder. The humming of the bees sounded loud, and when a stone rattled away from under her feet she was startled by the clatter.

Mrs. Pendennis was talkative, and some time passed before Lyd managed to escape from the store. She was crossing the grass by the inn lugging the heavy bag, when, without warning, she was carried back again into that world of cold and shadows. They *were* still shadows, but this time clear enough: men, and a few women and boys. The men were all bearded and they wore rough fishermen's jerseys, dark trousers, and great boots. The women had long skirts and, in a few cases, shawls. In their midst was the old woman from the cottage up the lane, being pushed along, drawn along, by grasping hands. The woman's terror filled Lyd, and in that brief flash of time the scene was nearly real, though seen against the opposite bank as something not quite solid. They were heading for the Cove, and it wasn't afternoon now, it was night. Yet the scene was brightly lit—by moonlight, she thought.

A car filled with tourists brought Lyd back to the present on the very edge of the grass. The time was no longer night, but hot afternoon, with heavy golden sunlight. The old woman and the crowd had gone.

When Lyd reached the cottage, her mother noticed at once that she was not herself.

"What is it, Lyd dear?" she asked. "Is it too hot? Maybe you ought to wear a hat. The sun isn't as clear now, but it's so heavy and thundery. I think it will end in a storm."

"I hate hats, and I like the heat."

"Well, have you a pain? A headache?"

"No, Mother, I haven't." Lyd laid her purchases out on the kitchen table.

"But sometimes you look . . . Don't you like this place, Lyd?"

"Of course I do. I love it."

"Well, we've only a few days more." Mrs. Allbright gave her daughter a baffled look and asked no more questions.

Lyd started off down the narrow path to the Cove. What were those people going to do to the old woman, who looked so nice and ordinary? Something suddenly twanged in her memory. An old woman, a cat, and a cottage. A garden . . . herbs, perhaps. She didn't look like a witch. She looked like someone's grandmother, kind and just like anyone else, in spite of her old-fashioned clothing. People hadn't believed in witches for a very long time, but how long? A hundred years perhaps. No, surely very much longer than that. People used to duck them in a deep pond, and if they floated they were considered innocent. Or was it the other way around? In any case, they usually drowned. People didn't learn to swim in those days. She had a dim idea if they *did* survive they were burned, because that proved they were possessed of unusual powers.

But what has she to do with me? Lyd asked herself, as she walked slowly on down the overgrown path.

Saul was busy, for there were a lot of tourists wanting boats and fishing gear, and Lyd kept knowledge of this new experience from him. The place was alive, crammed with cars, and he hardly glanced at her.

"Thank goodness you've come," he said. "It's one of my father's worst days. I don't know what I'd do without you."

Lyd ran around, taking money, helping to find gear, pushing out boats. This, she thought with relief, was life, something real and useful to do. But when a lull came to their activities she leaned on the wall, and gazed at the abandoned cottages and lofts.

In other days there must have been quite a lot of people living and working here, and fishing boats tied up at the quay. Trelonyan Cove must, in those times, have been much more remote than it was now, when cars came down the lane and a bus stopped by the signpost, ready to take people into Penzance. Penzance must, then, have seemed quite distant; perhaps the people here who made their living from the sea never visited it.

Once upon a time people were ignorant and superstitious, and sometimes they were wicked, without really knowing that they were wicked. They reacted to something they did not understand with violence, feeling that the only way to get around their fear was to eliminate the person they blamed. And there was no one to stop them.

But she was Lyd Allbright, even if she was adopted, and she lived in the 1970's. So why had she become caught up in what might be a very old tragedy? It was very muddling and frightening. Still, she had traveled a long way from the girl who had arrived in Cornwall, cramped with her brothers in the back of the old car, because now, in a strange way, she could take it in her stride, or thought she could. She would have to, anyway. There was no way out, short of leaving Trelonyan Cove.

They *would* be leaving in a few days, but Lyd was quite sure that she would know about the whole thing before those days had passed. She could not panic and beg to

be taken away. She was a person in her own right, a person
with a kind of mission. Somehow she was connected with
the past.

"Lyd!" shouted Saul. "Come on! What are you dream-
ing about?" And Lyd ran to help him, pushing away her
haunting thoughts.

The moon was getting toward the full, but that night,
as Lyd lay in bed, it was partly obscured by heavy clouds.
The air was windless and terribly hot, and far away
thunder rumbled.

Lyd's mother had already been in to kiss her good
night and had remarked that the room was hot. However, the window wouldn't open any further, and Lyd lay
on top of the sheet and blanket, hoping that there wasn't
going to be a storm.

She had always been scared of thunder. To the amuse-
ment of Tom and Jeff, she used to crawl into the space
under the stairs until a storm was over. That, of course,
had been when she was little. During the past few years
she had made a tremendous effort to be brave, because
she hated ridicule, even the most kindly sort, and Tom
and Jeff never intended to be unkind to her. It was *ab-
surd* to be scared of thunder when you were sixteen years
old and had coped with ghostly visions.

The night was much too hot for sleep, anyway. Lyd
slid off the bed and went to the window. The moon was
swinging up and she could see it now. It was yellowish
and looked curiously menacing. Then, as she watched,
another cloud passed slowly over it, so that for a short
time the world was almost dark.

She could hear the wash of the tide and a faint scuttling
in the bracken and foxgloves that might be rabbits.
Trelonyan Cove seemed remote from the rest of the

world, as remote as it must have been in those days she had glimpsed. At night no cars came down the lane, and no buses passed the signpost.

She tried not to think of what she had seen . . . that crowd of fisherfolk pushing and pulling the old woman. She fought to concentrate on the warm and pleasant things, like Saul kissing her in the green hollow and holding her on the heaving blue sea, but she was oppressed by Trelonyan under the cloudy moon.

Up on the other cliff, in the secret hollow, were the low ruins of the lost manor house. Up on her own cliff, only a short distance away around the corner, Mrs. Barstow must be alone in her cottage. Saul might be asleep. He was a down-to-earth person—or pretended to be—so maybe an eerie, thundery night wouldn't keep him awake.

Tom and Jeff had gone to bed at least thirty minutes ago, but her parents were still downstairs; she could hear the sound of their voices occasionally. Lyd was comforted to know that they were still awake in the pleasant, ordinary living room; then she was ashamed of her childish thought.

The moon floated free of cloud again, but looked more yellow than ever. The air had no movement in it at all. Lyd felt as if her lungs could not expand, could not take in any of the motionless air. Then suddenly a weird little wind sighed across the rocks and flowers and grass and, coming through the open window, lifted her hair off her hot forehead. It was certainly going to thunder.

She grew sleepy at last and went back to bed, where she fell into a deep sleep that lasted for several hours. Then she was awakened by brilliant flashes of lightning and crashes of thunder that drew nearer and nearer. Rain was falling in torrents, but falling straight, so that none came in through her open window.

Lyd realized that she was chilly and that she needed the warmth and protection of the bedclothes, so she dived under the sheet and blanket and lay shivering as the storm increased in violence.

The lightning showed even through her closed eyes and the bedclothes covering her head. The crashes were directly overhead, and Lyd longed to behave as she had as a child. She wanted to shout, "Mother!"

She didn't shout, but it was a wonderful relief when she heard her mother say, "Are you all right, Lyd? It's a bad storm. I don't ever remember a worse one."

"What time is it, Mother?" Lyd's head was still under the bedclothes.

"Four-thirty. The storm has been coming nearer for hours."

"I'm sure the cottage will be struck, or we'll be flooded out."

"We may be flooded out, but I hope we won't be struck by lightning. Shall I sit on your bed for a while and keep you company?"

"Oh, yes, please do." Lyd emerged for a moment. The storm seemed worse than ever; there was scarcely any lull between the thunder claps, but in a few seconds' respite she heard Tom's voice.

"What is it, Mother? A party? Can anyone join in?"

He plumped himself down heavily on the other side of Lyd's bed, and she raised her head to expose her hot face.

"Don't you dare laugh at me, Tom. It's an awful storm!"

"It certainly is," Tom agreed. "Hey, Jeff! Lyd requires company."

"Let's have some tea or something," suggested Jeff. "I'll make it."

"Cocoa," said his mother. "Shut Lyd's window, please, Jeff. The wind's getting up and the rain will come in."

"I hate a thunder wind," said Lyd. She felt ashamed of her fear and sat up. "Why don't we all go downstairs?" She'd feel safer in the living room, even though it was awful to have to look at the lightning.

They all went down the narrow, dark stairs, and Mrs. Allbright closed the draperies in the living room to shut out the worst of the blue glare. It wasn't so bad when there was company in the lighted room, and Lyd curled herself up in the armchair, gratefully sipping hot, sweet cocoa. Mr. Allbright joined them, saying there wasn't a hope of sleeping while the storm lasted, and it might be necessary to sweep out later.

"It's necessary now," said Jeff, coming in from the kitchen with the last of the cocoa. "The rain's beginning to seep under the door out there. I'll get the mop and bucket."

"I hope Mrs. Barstow is all right," said Mrs. Allbright. "It can't be very nice to be all alone in that isolated place."

"Oh!" Lyd jumped and slopped some of her drink as the light flickered. But it came on again bright as ever.

The storm lasted until daylight, and by then they were all working hard to keep the water down in the kitchen and bathroom. Rain was pouring down the slight slope and in at the back door, which had a gap underneath of about an inch. Although they tried to block up the space with newspapers and anything handy, some water still seeped through.

Lyd had recovered from her fear by then and was helping energetically. Wearing her old rubber boots, she mopped vigorously to give Jeff a rest. But at last the worst of the thunder died away, the lightning became more sporadic, and the rain fell more softly. Lyd looked out into the bleak, wet world outside, where the Cove lay below in the dim light and the harsh cliffs rose to the east.

"Back to bed!" said her mother, yawning. "We'll sleep for two or three hours and have breakfast late."

By nine-thirty, when they had nearly finished breakfast, the sun was shining and the drenched countryside was steaming as it began to dry. They had heard the news headlines, which told of severe storms all over Devon and Cornwall, of telephone lines damaged, and of people without electricity. Roads had been flooded and blocked by fallen trees and other debris.

"Well, we've been luckier than most," said Mr. Allbright. "Our electricity is all right."

Saul came up just as they rose from the table, to see how they had fared during the night. He told them that the stream had overflowed its banks and caused trouble at the inn and post office, and that all the telephones were out of order—the public one and those at the inn and post office.

"Mrs. Pendennis thinks the lines were struck," he said. "Mr. Pendennis is going to drive somewhere until he finds one that works, then he'll tell the telephone people. At the moment we're cut off."

"Well, I don't suppose it matters," Mr. Allbright said easily. "Not unless there's an emergency. Couldn't he tell the man who drives the mail van?"

"He hasn't come yet. Mr. Pendennis thinks he'd better go and see what's been happening. The lane could be blocked by a tree or something."

"We were sweeping the water out," Lyd told him. "There's a gap under the back door."

"How is the car?" Saul asked.

"Oh, I saw the storm coming and put a huge plastic

sheet over the old thing," Mr. Allbright explained. "It was well covered."

Saul went off, saying he had to bail out some of the boats, and Lyd promised to join him as soon as the household tasks were finished. Mr. Allbright, Tom, and Jeff decided to take a boat and go fishing again. That was the thing they enjoyed most, and the family couldn't get *really* tired of eating fish during the next few days. The price of fish was so high in Bristol that they didn't often have it at home.

"Why don't you come with us, Lyd?" asked Tom. "You haven't been yet, and it's great in the boat. You've done plenty of work with boats and it seems silly not to have been out in one."

"But I promised to help Saul," Lyd pointed out.

"Well, help him for a short time. We aren't going yet. We can catch plenty of fish in an hour or so, usually."

Lyd felt close to her family that morning, after the comradeship of the night, so she agreed. It would be nice to be out on the sea. She ran down the path and did some bailing out with Saul. He said he was going to repair one of the boats under his father's instructions as soon as the bailing out was finished. No cars had come down to the Cove, so it was a good chance.

When her father and brothers came from the cottage, Lyd climbed cheerfully into their boat. She sat in the stern and trailed her fingers in the sea, looking down into the clear, blue-green depths. Everything was peaceful and beautiful, and she found it interesting to see Trelonyan Cove from just a few hundred yards out, which was much nearer than the Scilly Isles steamer had been. Now the morning light lay full on the Cove, although the deep valley beyond still looked deep and secret. When she looked up she could see Tamarisk Cottage and Mrs. Barstow's cottage. Mrs. Barstow was on the cliff, spreading sheets out to dry on the gorse bushes, and she waved. Her figure looked small and far away, but recognizable.

Time passed quickly and they had a good catch. At twelve-thirty the tide was high and they were able to take the boat right in instead of going to one of the flights of narrow, slippery steps that descended from the quay. But while they were still a few yards out from the stony shore below the abandoned cottages, Lyd, who had been perfectly happy and relaxed, had a terrible moment of black cold, when her whole being seemed engulfed in fear.

CHAPTER TEN

The Decision

Lyd cried out, without knowing that she had done so, and her father and brothers turned to her in amazement and shock. Dead white, she was clutching the gunwale with hands so tense that the bones stuck out.

"Lyd! What is it?" Tom demanded. He was nearest, and he tried to grasp her, but she shook him off.

"They are—doing something awful!" she gulped.

"Who? Lyd, there's nothing. Are you seasick? You couldn't be. It was as calm as a millpond."

"They're wicked! They don't know what they're doing. . . . She isn't a witch. Just nice and ordinary. I *know* that!"

Then Lyd came to herself, shivering and shaking. She was in the boat with her father and Tom and Jeff, and Saul and Mrs. Barstow were standing together on the shore.

When the boat grounded on the stones, she could hardly stand and had to be helped. Mr. Allbright was pale-faced and utterly bewildered.

"What happened to her?" he asked. "Lyd, why did you say those things?"

"What did she say?" asked Mrs. Barstow. "Come here, Lyd. You're all right, dear. You're with us."

"I don't know. A lot of nonsense about people being wicked, and about someone not being a witch," Mr. Allbright said. "My wife said she thought this place sometimes had a strange effect on Lyd, and I thought she was talking nonsense. But I saw and heard this for myself."

"It was nothing," said Lyd. The fear had gone, and she was herself again, though weak and shaky still. She knew she had given herself away fully at last, and shrank from the consequences.

"No, it was something," Mrs. Barstow said quietly to Lyd's father.

"She looked like someone in a trance," said Mr. Allbright. "I've read about such things and seen people on television. I never thought I'd believe it, though. Lyd, I'm going to get to the bottom of this."

"You'll have to tell them now, Lyd," said Mrs. Barstow, and Lyd glared at her resentfully. Saul stood silent, looking desperately worried.

"Tell us what?" asked Lyd's father.

"You ought to know. . . . I told Lyd so, days ago. I only know myself because I saw her like that on another occasion. This isn't a good place for her. You ought to take her away."

"But a child of mine. . . . I don't understand."

Mrs. Barstow saw that he had forgotten that Lyd wasn't literally his child, that she was not a member of the family by blood. It was going to be hard for the everyday, sensible Allbrights to grasp what had been happening to Lyd. But they would have to try to understand. Their reactions now would show, perhaps, how much they loved and felt for her.

"Let's go up to your cottage," Mrs. Barstow suggested. "May I come, too?"

"Of course," said Mr. Allbright. "I intend to understand this strange business if it's the last thing I do."

"You may find it difficult," said Mrs. Barstow.

There seemed to be no escape. Lyd gave Saul one imploring glance, but he avoided her gaze. There was nothing he could say, anyway; she had to go through with it.

They climbed in single file up the steep path. Mr. Allbright went first, then Lyd, followed by Mrs. Barstow. Tom and Jeff, silent, and looking baffled and upset, brought up the rear.

Mrs. Barstow spoke of the storm until they reached the cottage, where Mrs. Allbright was looking out for them. She stared in surprise and alarm when she saw the expressions on all their faces. Lyd felt better, but she was still pale, and she was really worried now that the moment of reckoning had come. They'd be so mad. . . . They certainly wouldn't believe her. She wished, suddenly and passionately, that she had reached that great age of twenty, for then she wouldn't have to account for herself.

The meal was forgotten, though the table was laid and potatoes and cabbage from the garden were cooking. Tom and Jeff were extremely curious, but they kept out of the way as Mr. and Mrs. Allbright, Mrs. Barstow, and Lyd sat down in the living room. Mrs. Barstow was calm and helped Lyd to be calm, but she also saw to it that Lyd told the whole strange story.

At first Lyd's father continued to look bewildered, for he found such a tale hard to grasp, and harder to believe. But Mrs. Allbright was quicker, more responsive.

"I knew there was something," she said. "I knew it from that first moment in the car, when we were coming down the lane. I've heard of such things, but Lyd. . . . Is she psychic? A medium or something?"

"She may be," said Mrs. Barstow. "Though I gather she's shown no sign of it before, and it does seem to be just this one thing . . . something that happened in Trelonyan."

"But Lyd does have imagination," Mrs. Allbright went on. "She's clever and she thinks of things. Couldn't it just have been . . . ?"

"I wish you wouldn't talk about me as if I weren't here!" complained Lyd.

"Of course, you must be right," Mr. Allbright said to his wife, grasping eagerly at a rational explanation. "Something about this place has made her use her imagination." He didn't sound angry, but merely puzzled and worried.

"Well, whatever it is," said Mrs. Barstow, "I think you should take her away. She's coped with it remarkably well, but I don't think she should be under any more strain. Oh, you needn't frown at me, Lyd. It wouldn't be childish and silly to go away."

Mr. Allbright looked at his daughter, remembering the countless times in years past when she had been unreasonably scared and had said so. As she grew older she had tried to hide her feelings, and over this last thing. . . . Yes, Lyd had grown up. It was all extraordinary, and troubling, and he didn't believe for a moment that she had really seen and felt anything in Trelonyan. Yet during those moments in the boat. . . .

He came to an immediate decision.

"I think you're right," he said to Mrs. Barstow. "We can't stay here any longer if it's bad for Lyd, for whatever reason. Of course we'd have been going, anyway, in two or three days, but we'll pack and leave this evening. We'll find a place that does bed and breakfast in Penzance and start home in the morning."

Lyd stared at her father. One side of her was filled

with relief and joy, for he must love her very much, he must care terribly, to speak like that, to make such a plan. But the other side, the part of her that was grown up, was shocked and resentful. She wasn't a child, who was spoiling their vacation by being taken away from danger. And there wasn't any danger . . . maybe painful knowledge, that was all.

"But I don't want to go," she protested. "It's good of you, Dad. I know you think it's for the best, but it isn't necessary."

"It's necessary," said Mr. Allbright grimly. "There's enough money to spend a couple of nights at cheap places on the way home. We'll have to clean up the cottage and leave it neat, but we'll be off not later than six o'clock this evening."

"We'll manage that all right," agreed his wife. "It *is* best, Lyd dear. Don't look so stricken."

"Oh, all right," Lyd muttered ungraciously. She hadn't learned quite the end of the story. She wasn't sure what had happened to the old woman. Of course it was wonderful that her father was so concerned for her; it meant that she wholly belonged and must be protected. He wouldn't take any risks for her, even if she would take them for herself. But what on earth would Tom and Jeff say?

Tom and Jeff said very little. Told most of the story by their mother after lunch, they could only clearly understand that they were leaving because the place didn't suit Lyd. The talk of ghostly visions bewildered them, all the more so because their father and mother seemed to believe what had happened. They were not resentful, though they were hopelessly puzzled. They liked Trelonyan Cove and had been looking forward to their last days there, but they were an equable pair of boys, and spending two nights on their way back would mean that their holiday was not really curtailed.

"It's rum about Lyd, though," Tom said to Jeff, as they set about packing up their possessions.

"She's a queer girl," Jeff agreed. "Having visions. . . . I don't get it. But she was awfully strange in the boat. I was really scared; I've never seen anything like it before."

"Or heard. Witches, she said! What have witches got to do with it? This old woman she thinks she has seen—"

"They ducked them in the village pond, didn't they?"

"Well, there's no pond here. Though, of course, plenty of water. Do you think that Saul can have been stuffing her up with local stories? Anything might fire Lyd's imagination."

"I don't know. Could be. Anyway, Dad's made up his mind. He won't take risks where Lyd's concerned. He dotes on her, more than he does on us."

"Well, fair enough," Tom remarked. "She's a girl, and I suppose girls are more sensitive."

"But," said Jeff, who was observant, "she has changed lately. She seems much older. Do you think she really likes Saul Treporth?"

Tom was taken aback, because he was the one who had a girl friend. Until then he had never thought of it.

"You may be right," he allowed. "But we're leaving, anyway. Come on, hurry up. Mother says we're to help clean the whole place out before we go, and there's the car to pack as well. Plenty to do."

Lyd, silent and not quite sure what to think or feel, worked hard with the rest. She didn't dare let herself think of Saul, for that way, she knew, pain would lie. They might meet again, but it was not certain.

She packed her own clothes and helped her mother to put things back where they had found them on their arrival at the cottage. By five o'clock the car was packed and they had had tea. Saul hadn't appeared and Lyd's heart was heavy. She *had* to see him to say good-bye, and to tell him he could come and visit them in Bristol if he wanted to.

"Mother," she said. "I must go down and speak to Saul."

"Of course you must," her mother agreed. "Go now. I hope you'll see him again. You did say he had an uncle who could give him a lift to Bristol. You like him, don't you, Lyd?"

"Yes, I do." Lyd went quickly down the steep path and came out by the Cove. The fine afternoon had brought a lot of tourists and the place was brilliantly lighted by the sun and wholly alive, although the deserted cottages and lofts were a reminder that, with the coming of dusk, the Cove would belong to itself again.

Saul saw her and came running. "Oh, Lyd, I wanted to see you. I wanted to know what had happened, but I thought it would be better to wait."

"We're going away . . . in less than an hour," Lyd told him. She watched his face. A mixed expression showed in his eyes . . . regret, relief.

He said, "So your father decided?"

"Yes, he thinks it's best. I—I'm glad he wants to do what he thinks will be good for me, but I don't want to go, Saul. We're spending the night in Penzance, and maybe two more nights on the way."

Saul took her hand and looked down at her.

"So it's good-bye? I'm sorry, Lyd, but it would have come soon, anyway. It's been fun . . . more than fun. You've helped a lot, and I'm glad we met. I'll see you again. I'll write to you."

"Will you?"

"Yes. I've never had anyone to write letters to before."

Maybe he would explain in a letter what he had not been willing to tell her—if, of course, there was anything to tell. Lyd turned and ran back to the path; if she stayed any longer she might cry, and that would be shameful. She was fighting back the tears all the way up the steep path. It was *awful* to part from someone she liked so much, and with a vague mystery hanging over the relationship. Never before had she felt such heartache.

When she reached the cottage she found consternation. The car wouldn't start. All the efforts of Tom and Mr. Allbright were unavailing. The engine just wouldn't show any sign of life.

"But it was perfectly dry after the storm," Jeff remarked.

"It's the battery, I'm sure," said his father. "I'll have to get someone to come from a garage. I'll go down and telephone now."

"Hope they've fixed the phones, then," said Tom.

Lyd stood out on the grassland by the car, feeling the hot late afternoon sunlight on her back. If they couldn't leave, she would see Saul again. Maybe it was fate.

Mr. Allbright walked down to Trelonyan and found that the telephones had not been fixed. Mrs. Pendennis leaned on the counter in her leisurely way, though it was nearly closing time, and explained.

"You see, Mr. Allbright," she said, "half of Western Cornwall was cut off. That's what they told my husband when he finally found a telephone that worked this morning. They said it might be tomorrow before our phones are working, and I'm afraid that's how it's going to be. Ted went as far as Newlyn before he found a telephone that was all right. He had quite a job getting out of our lane. Right near the top a tree had come down and there were branches all over the road. The man who drives the mail van had started to clear them, and some road workers came along and helped. It's been quite a day, what with being so busy this afternoon." She was all set to chatter on, but Mr. Allbright, dismayed and impatient, cut in.

"But we'd decided to leave this evening, and everything's packed. Now the car won't go, and I'm sure it's the battery. I wonder if your husband would lend me his car to go and find a garage." But as he spoke he remembered that he had not seen the car parked in its usual place.

"Ted's gone into Penzance to a meeting and won't be back until late." Mrs. Pendennis knew nothing about Lyd's visions and was greatly puzzled by the decision to leave Tamarisk Cottage so suddenly.

Mr. Allbright stood in the tiny shop, baffled and upset. The Clarks had no car; they relied on the bus. Mrs. Barstow had no car, either. Where was the nearest garage? he wondered. There might be one in Paul, but it was miles away, and there was probably one in Mousehole, even farther. He could maybe borrow Mrs. Barstow's bicycle, if she was home by now, but that would take a long time. He was sure the car needed a new battery, an expensive business, and possibly delaying even when he *did* get in touch with a garage. In addition, all the bed-and-breakfast places would be full by seven o'clock.

They'd just have to stay another night. That couldn't make much difference to Lyd. She must go to bed early. They'd all go to bed early, for they needed sleep after the wakeful night of the storm.

"Well, there's nothing to be done until tomorrow, I suppose," he said to Mrs. Pendennis, and left her more puzzled than ever. She hated to be kept in the dark about anything, and if there was some kind of trouble, perhaps she could help. She more or less made up her mind to go up to Tamarisk Cottage later, but as it happened, she grew absorbed in a magazine after supper, and then felt it was too late.

Meanwhile, Mr. Allbright climbed slowly back to the cottage and imparted his news. They carried some of the things back into the house and Mrs. Allbright planned supper. Luckily there was plenty of food; they had been going to take some of it with them.

Lyd's feelings were a trifle mixed, but the main one was a deep sense of relief. She knew now that her father would do what he thought best for her, would sacrifice the rest of the family for her sake. He had been understanding to the limits of his capacity, and he was not angry with her at all. But his efforts had failed, and so here they were still in Trelonyan as the shadows began to slant across the Cove.

Those moments in the boat had been awful, but now that the fear had passed, she was more than ever certain that it had not been hers. And fear once removed was easier to bear. She had *seen* nothing then; perhaps she had to see something more before she went away. Not in daylight, but in moonlight.

Before it was anywhere near dark, the full moon was swinging up over the scene, and tonight it was clear and pale. It was a most beautiful evening, calm and still, and Lyd didn't want to go to bed. She leaned on the bank, gazing downward, wishing that she had gone to see Saul again, and thinking, almost sadly, that she might never see the Cove again. It was a strange, secret place, with old horrors, but in a peculiar way she felt she belonged there, as part of its grimness and remoteness, part of its

past. Tomorrow they would probably sleep out of Cornwall, in some place that was not haunted by old
mysteries.

In a way the evening had been awkward, for she hadn't
known what to say to anyone, but she was curiously happy
now, almost at peace, apart from wanting Saul.

She gave a jump when a voice said quietly, "Lyd!"

It was Saul. He was standing just behind her. She was
so glad to see him that she almost flung herself into his
arms, but stopped herself in time.

"Mrs. Pendennis told me you hadn't gone yet," he
said. "I was taking a walk and she looked out and saw me."

"No, the car wouldn't start. Dad thinks it's the battery,
and the phones aren't working."

He sat on the bank beside her, with the moonlight on
his face "I'm glad . . . and sorry. I thought you were away
and—and safe."

"Safe from what?" she asked. "I'm all right, Saul, and
everyone's been wonderful to me."

"From your visions, or whatever they are," he said.

"Lyd, we're all going to bed. You must come in at
once," her mother called. "Oh, hello, Saul! We haven't
gone, you see. Lyd can speak to you in the morning."

Saul said good night and went off down the path. Lyd
followed her mother indoors.

"Mother," she said quietly, "I didn't mean . . . I didn't
want to spoil it for everyone else."

"It's all right, love. Don't worry about it. It may be
better to go. Get a good sleep."

But Lyd couldn't sleep. The room was bright with
moonlight and she heard the sigh of the rising tide. She
tossed and turned for hours and knew it must be almost
midnight. The cottage was utterly silent; all the others
were asleep.

The tide was high in the Cove and the whole world was brilliantly silvered by the light of the full moon when Lyd sat up in bed and very slowly and carefully slid to the floor. She went to the window. Outside, the black-and-silver world looked infinitely peaceful. Almost without thinking, without planning, she swiftly put on a few clothes: shorts, a cotton blouse, rubber-soled sandals. Something was drawing her outdoors, into the moonlight. She realized dimly that there was no escape. She had to know.

CHAPTER ELEVEN

What Happened in Moonlight

Lyd found it easy enough to leave her bedroom by way of the window, though she had to wriggle a little to get through, because it didn't open very wide. She crouched cautiously on the roof of the bathroom, feeling with her toe for a narrow ledge she had seen by the pipe. Then she was gripping the pipe and sliding down. She reached the grass with only the faintest of plops, but heard Collie give a faint bark, quickly hushed. Thank goodness they shut Collie indoors when they went to bed!

It was almost unbearably beautiful. Never before in her life had she been out in the country in the middle of the night. Even at home in Bristol she was almost always home by ten-thirty, unless she went to a party, and then someone always drove her home.

She ought to have been scared, but she was not; her emotions were not nearly so easy to explain. There was a sense of inevitability, a feeling of curiosity, and certainly a twinge of guilt, for her parents would be upset if they knew, and she had worried them enough.

She was sure that what she was definitely to witness soon would be dreadful, but at that point she did not think it would affect her in a personal way. In fact, she would find it harder to bear if she never knew for certain what had happened in Trelonyan Cove a long time ago.

To have any kind of present-day company was clearly impossible. No one—not Saul, nor Mrs. Barstow, nor her own family—had seen or felt anything when they were with her on those other occasions. The thing was being reenacted for Lyd alone. No, that wasn't right. She thought Mrs. Barstow was correct about the event being something that went on and on, because it was imprinted on the very air of the place. But even though she believed it had happened long, long ago, in a poorer-educated, crueler age than her own, she, Lyd Allbright, belonged to it somehow.

Come to think of it, though, she said to herself as she started down the path, terrible things still happen. People can still do awful things.

She went very slowly, stopping to look and listen and to breathe the sweet air. Caution was necessary, in any case, because, in spite of the moonlight, parts of the narrow path were dark and she could easily trip over a stone or a root.

Once she felt a sudden surge of fear and nearly went back, but the urge passed. The girl who had always been afraid had learned courage of a high order during the days in Cornwall. Besides, she didn't seem to have much choice.

The tide was at its highest and the water was silver-clear. Most of the Treporths' boats were drawn up on the stones on the inland side of the Cove, but a few were floating, tied up near the two flights of steps that went down from the quay.

Very slowly, but without hesitation, Lyd set foot on the

smooth old stones of the quay. Then she stopped and looked around, cold and aware, but nothing had gone black and she was still conscious of being herself.

But now everything was different. More cottages ringed the shore, and they extended to the very foot of the opposite cliff. There were still lofts or warehouses, but cottages stood in front of them, almost on the stony shore. The boats, some of them anchored away from the quay, were different. They were fishing boats with masts and furled sails.

Then she saw the people. Some of them were huddled in groups in the moonlight, but others, she felt rather than saw, were cowering in the doorways or behind the closed windows of the cottages. She swung back to face the quay, and there she saw more people quite clearly, their not wholly substantial faces revealed in the brilliant light. They were between her and the old beacon, which now looked new.

Suddenly she forgot everything else as a familiar figure appeared in the middle of the moving crowd on the quay . . . the old woman. As Lyd watched, cold all over with horror, many hands thrust and pushed at the old woman until she fell over the high edge of the quay into the deep water.

The crowd stood there watching, unmoving, and apparently shouting, but although Lyd could see their mouths opening and shutting, she heard no sound. Then she saw the cat, halfway between her and the people on the quay. Someone else saw it too, a big man in a rough jersey and trousers, and fishermen's boots. He scooped the animal up in his hands and threw it after the old woman.

Lyd tried to run forward then, irrationally intending

to help, but she found that she could not move. She saw a young man snatch up a stone and hurl it at the old woman as she struggled in the water. His face was clear in the moonlight. It was Saul.

Lyd screamed then, and kept on screaming, eyes tightly shut, until Mrs. Barstow came running and seized her and held her. From far away Lyd recognized her voice.

"Lyd! Why are you here? What happened? I thought you'd gone away. Lyd!"

Lyd clung to her, burying her face in the artist's smock, which smelled of paint.

"We couldn't go, because the car wouldn't start, and there are no telephones. It was all because of the thunderstorm. And I wasn't really sorry, for I had to know. But it was worse than I thought. I couldn't bear it. Oh, Mrs. Barstow, they drowned her and the cat, and Saul . . . *Saul* threw a stone! He was laughing. . . . I saw him clearly. Oh, how could he be so wicked?"

"No one was there, Lyd," Mrs. Barstow said quietly. "Saul certainly wasn't."

"But I *saw* him! I did, really. I couldn't have imagined that. I thought Saul was good and kind. But he was there in the crowd. He bent down and picked up a stone; then he threw it."

"Lyd, you must believe me. This whole place was silent and peaceful . . . to me. I couldn't sleep, so I came down to paint the scene by moonlight. My easel is over there, by the first loft. You didn't see me, but I saw you arrive. And Saul is asleep at home, unless your screams woke him up. Yes, here he comes now, from the cottage."

Lyd stared in amazement. Saul was crossing the stone bridge, wearing pajamas and sandals. She shrank back as he approached, and Saul stopped, looking puzzled and hurt.

"I heard. . . . What's the matter, Lyd? And why are you looking at me like that?"

He hadn't been dressed like that before, but—

"Saul . . . I never thought you could, but I *saw* you myself. You threw a stone and it hit her."

"What's she talking about?" Saul asked Mrs. Barstow. He took a step or two toward Lyd and she moved back involuntarily.

"She saw what happened here a long time ago, I think, and she insists you threw a stone at the old woman. I believe they must have drowned her in the Cove."

At that moment Mr. Allbright arrived, with his shirt and trousers obviously hastily put on.

"I found Lyd wasn't in bed, so I came down and heard her screaming," he explained breathlessly. Lyd rushed to him and tried to explain, but the words came out incoherently. She was still far from her normal self. The only words that were wholly clear were her repeated insistences that Saul had been there. Somewhere, deep within her, she was conscious of a feeling of heartbreak. Saul was lost. She had never really known him.

Saul was dead white in the moonlight. "I wasn't there," he said. "Don't be a fool, Lyd! That wasn't me. I think you must have seen my great-great-uncle. Or maybe another great. You see, we lived here once, my family, I mean. I didn't want to tell you. It was a long time ago."

Everyone stared at him, then Mrs. Barstow, who was the least involved, said calmly, "Lyd asked me if I thought you knew anything. She had begun to think you were keeping something from her. Didn't you, Lyd?"

Lyd gasped and nodded, trying to think clearly.

"You took me away from the library, and once or twice you looked and sounded strange. But it *was* you, Saul. I saw your eyes and your whole body."

"Oh, come off it, Lyd!" Saul, much shaken, tried to strike a sensible note. "You were right. I did know something, but not the whole story. I just knew that something awful had been done here once, and that a member of our family had been involved. My father told me when we came here, but he said it was all forgotten countless years ago by everyone but the family. He heard part of the story from his father, who had it from *his* father, who lived to be well over ninety. I just knew it was one of those last witch things, when villagers got all worked up and superstitious over someone they thought had evil powers."

"She was not evil," said Lyd in a muffled voice. "You shouldn't have thrown the stone."

"Lyd, don't you understand?" Saul demanded urgently. "It wasn't me. I was sound asleep. And can I really be blamed for something an ancestor did? It wasn't even someone in the direct line. It was the younger son, when he was seventeen or eighteen. That much they always insisted on. He ran away to sea a short time later and came to a bad end in some foreign port. *My* family—my ancestors, everyone apart from that boy—was against the whole thing. They never believed she was a witch, but the feeling was too strong."

"Are you sure you didn't tell Lyd any of this?" Mr. Allbright had been listening in bewilderment. He grasped now at the only sensible explanation.

"I didn't tell her anything, Mr. Allbright. Lyd's right. I didn't want her to find out. Though actually there isn't anything mentioned in any book I could find in the library. I suppose it was all pretty well hushed up, and this was a very remote place. It couldn't have happened otherwise. Anyway, the Treporths left the place after what had happened and settled in Newlyn, and none of them ever talked about it outside the family. It was a secret, passed on."

"But you came back?" Lyd's mind was working again, and she wondered if Saul would ever forgive her for shrinking from him, blaming him.

"We had the chance of this cottage very cheaply after Dad's accident. He said I'd better know the story when we came, but told me to keep it to myself. And naturally I wasn't exactly proud of it. Then *you* came, Lyd, with your talk of cold places and visions. I was horrified when I began to believe you really could see and feel things. But don't blame me. I had nothing to do with it. It was a long time ago, early in the last century."

"I don't, honestly. I understand now," Lyd said.

Mr. Allbright had had enough, and he knew his wife would be desperately worried by their continued absence.

"I don't understand a word of it," he said brusquely. "Come back to bed, Lyd. We'll leave in the morning, just as soon as we can get the car fixed. You shouldn't have come out in the middle of the night. It was a crazy thing to do."

"I couldn't help it, you know," Lyd said, as they climbed the path. "Honest, I couldn't. Something made me go down to the Cove, and now it's all explained . . . in a kind of way. But I do wish I hadn't seen that boy who looked so much like Saul."

"It's a most extraordinary story," said her father, who felt he would never get a grasp on the real world again. He was beaten by Saul's statement that something really had happened in Trelonyan Cove a long time ago and that the Treporth family had been involved. All the same, Lyd *must* have read about it in a book. That was the only rational explanation he could think of.

But the next morning Lyd insisted she had never read one word about Trelonyan in a book. She was rather ashamed, but perfectly calm by then, for she thought the whole thing was over. Her heart ached when she thought of Saul, for he might never forgive her for thinking he could behave so wickedly. She hoped *she* would one day forget the way his ancestor had looked in the moonlight, laughing and thoughtless, throwing that stone.

The telephone lines were repaired by ten o'clock and Mr. Allbright got in touch with a garage. A mechanic arrived thirty minutes later, bringing a new battery, which was a dreadful extra expense. But the car then ran sweetly, and they made preparations for almost immediate departure.

Saul did not appear, but Mrs. Barstow did. She was relieved to see Lyd, looking fairly relaxed and well, carrying things out to the car.

Mrs. Barstow drew Mr. and Mrs. Allbright to one side. "Lyd looks all right," she began.

"I think she is, more or less," said Mrs. Allbright. She certainly didn't look all right herself after hours of sleeplessness and worry. "But now she says she wishes she knew more, just how it happened, because the old woman looked so nice. And I'm afraid she's worrying about Saul, though she won't speak of that. Maybe Lyd will never be quite settled unless she can learn more about that long-ago affair, but there seems to be no way of understanding. Saul told her he doesn't think it's in any books."

"There is a way," said Mrs. Barstow, "and I hope you'll let her take it. I know it's asking a lot, for I'm sure you'd all sooner forget what happened, but I do think it may be best for Lyd. She has a questing mind and she deserves more knowledge."

"But how can she get it?" Mrs. Allbright asked, puzzled.

"When you leave here you could make a short detour to St. Buryan. There's a cottage near the church, where a Mr. Tregowan lives—Professor Tregowan, really. He's over ninety, but very alert mentally, and still deeply interested in Cornish matters. I want you to let Lyd tell him her story. I think he will then tell her something she will want to hear."

Mr. Allbright frowned. "I'll not have Lyd's strange moods and experiences made public property," he said angrily. "Too many people know already. We're heading straight home, maybe staying one night on the way. That's all I can afford now that I've paid for that battery."

"Professor Tregowan would keep her secret. He says he is too old to write any more, and he sees few strangers. I only met him by accident a couple of weeks ago. Yesterday afternoon I went to see him again. Without telling him Lyd's name or anything about her, I told him a young girl had been having experiences in the Cove. I asked him if anything had ever happened there to justify them. He told me to look at a certain grave in the churchyard, and he also read me parts of an old diary. The diary was left to him, among other Cornish papers, by a very old friend who died recently at the age of ninety-five. The friend thought he might be interested, as he lives not far from Trelonyan."

"I still don't think—"

"The Professor has no idea how the diary came into his friend's hands," Mrs. Barstow went on, ignoring the interruption. "It was kept by a Mary Trelonyan, who lived

at the Manor here. He would read the important parts to
Lyd. He said he would, if she cared to go."

"He'll think Lyd mad," Mr. Allbright said slowly.

"He's so old that nothing is too strange for him to believe. Lyd will like him and trust him."

"I still think she could forget it now."

"Maybe she will, as time goes on, but don't you think
you should let her choose? She's sixteen and must soon
get into the habit of making her own decisions."

Mr. Allbright hesitated. He liked Mrs. Barstow well
enough, but she wasn't their kind of person. An artist,
living alone. Clever . . . too clever. And Lyd's welfare was
none of her business.

But Mrs. Allbright said, "Maybe we should. It's all so
peculiar, and not a pretty story as far as I can make out."

"Far from pretty, but such things did happen. This was
a very late case, but the place was terribly remote, even
up to the early years of this present century. Please let me
explain to Lyd."

When they agreed she called Lyd, who advanced
slowly. Seen close to, she was paler than usual and had
dark circles under her eyes. When she heard the suggestion her eyes grew eager.

"Saul told me about that old man, but he said he
wouldn't know anything. But he has a diary? Mary Trelonyan . . . you mean she lived at the lost manor house?
Oh, if I could hear it as a story I might *think* of it as a
story, and not as something I actually saw."

"All right, you can go," her father said. "We'll drop
you there and take a drive while you're speaking to him.
But you mustn't stay long."

"His housekeeper guards him carefully," said Mrs.
Barstow. "She won't let any visitor stay long." Then she
asked, "Are you going to see Saul before you leave, Lyd?"

Lyd went paler than ever. She was scared of seeing Saul after what had happened in the moonlight, but it would be even worse not to do so.

"I—yes."

"Walk down with me then."

Mrs. Barstow said her farewells to the Allbrights, then she and Lyd started off down the path to the Cove.

CHAPTER TWELVE

The Diary of Mary Trelonyan

Mrs. Barstow and Lyd walked one behind the other, not saying much. But near the bottom of the path Lyd said, with some difficulty:

"You've been . . . very kind. I don't know what I would have done without you."

"I've enjoyed knowing you, Lyd," Mrs. Barstow said warmly. "Maybe you'll write and tell me what you think about the diary."

"I will. Of course I will."

Then Lyd saw Saul. He was standing on the stones, talking to some tourists, but when he saw her he walked forward. It was an awkward, painful moment for Lyd, and she was glad when Mrs. Barstow turned and went quickly up her own path.

Saul, however, did not seem to find it awkward. He took both her hands.

"I suppose it really is good-bye this time, Lyd. For a time, anyway. I'll come to Bristol. We'll meet again, you know."

"Oh, Saul!" Lyd stared up at him. "I . . . I do have to say I'm sorry for the way I behaved last night."

"Nothing to be sorry about. *I'm* sorry I didn't tell you, but I really did shrink from it."

Relieved, her heart warm again, Lyd poured out the news about the diary and how she was going to see Professor Tregowan.

"It's strange that he has it, isn't it, Saul? You don't mind my going? I won't tell him about your ancestor, or mention you."

"I don't mind. Maybe you'd better know all there is to know. Perhaps I'll even go and see him myself one day. I'd rather like to know more, too, now it's all out in the open. But I won't tell my father or anyone here. How can I? Too strange a tale." He gave her a light kiss on her cheek and turned her back toward the path.

In a few minutes they were all in the car and driving away up the lane. As they passed the "cold place" for the last time, Lyd felt nothing. She almost missed the sensation, frightening as it had so often been. But it seemed that the ghosts—the shadows—had gone.

They found Professor Tregowan's cottage without difficulty; it was quite large, built of granite, and was standing in a flowery garden. In the garden sat the old man himself, reading a newspaper. He was quite handsome and didn't look his great age. His hair shone silver, and his face was healthily pink. Lyd knew at once that she wouldn't be shy with him.

She wriggled from the car, and her family watched her go through the gate. Tom and Jeff were silent, more puzzled than ever by the turn events had taken. Then the car drove away.

"Good morning, Professor Tregowan," Lyd said, as she approached the old man. "I'm Lyd Allbright. Mrs. Barstow told me to come. We're leaving Trelonyan now. My family are coming back for me in a short time."

Professor Tregowan had not been told the name of the girl who claimed she had seen and felt things in Trelonyan Cove, but he knew at once that this was she. She was younger than he had imagined, so small and dark in her short red dress. A real little Celt, she looked. Mrs. Barstow hadn't explained that.

"You want to talk to me?" he asked, and Lyd nodded earnestly.

"Yes, I do, please. If it won't bore you, and if you'll promise not to tell anyone. You see, I do so want to hear Mary Trelonyan's diary."

The old man eyed her thoughtfully. Pretty girl, or would be in a year or two. And intelligent. It wasn't often he had attractive young visitors, and Mrs. Barstow's story had aroused his curiosity.

"I promise," he said, "and it certainly won't bore me. Shall we go indoors? The diary is in my study."

He seized his stick and walked slowly up the path to the cottage door, with Lyd following. The elderly housekeeper at once appeared in the small hallway, but the Professor waved her away.

"I have a visitor and don't want to be disturbed."

Lyd then told him her story. She told it clearly and well until she reached the last part, what had happened in the moonlight. She found that much harder. But she reached the end at last, having left out only two things: She did not tell him Saul's surname, or mention the fact that she had recognized his face on his shadowy ancestor. That was Saul's secret, and she would let him tell it himself, if he ever sought out the Professor. She thought she had included everything else, even the slight experience in Marazion, though it seemed unimportant.

The Professor listened without comment, nodding occasionally. She was not watching him all the time, so did not notice his start of surprise at the mention of Marazion. He did not seem to her startled or unbelieving, but Lyd added when she had finished the tale:

"Truly I never read about it. I don't know why *I* saw it all. I had never heard or read anything about it at all."

"You hardly could have," said the old man, "for very little is known. There are a few mentions in old papers, scholarly works on the belief in witchcraft. But you wouldn't have come across those. And I kept the diary entirely to myself until I read parts of it to Mrs. Barstow yesterday. Maybe it should be published. It's interesting and it does shed light on those times. But I won't be the one to do it." He paused. "Do you know, the most remarkable thing in your story is that you felt slightly 'possessed' in Marazion."

"Oh, why?" Lyd was bewildered.

"Well, that you never could have known. It's only a mention in the diary and, even then, not a fact. But something took you to the traces of a cottage there above the sea. It's outside my experience all right, but I think you were possessed."

Lyd was relieved, rather than alarmed. He certainly did believe her.

"But," she said, "there's something more than old papers, isn't there? Mrs. Barstow said there was a grave in the churchyard. *Her* grave, is it? Not Mary Trelonyan's?"

"Oh, Mary's there, and her father and mother, and her brother and his wife. And the few who came after them. Mary died in 1840, at the age of sixty-six. By 1870 the family had died out, and Trelonyan Manor was empty. There was never a church or graveyard in Trelonyan, so they were all brought here. But the interesting grave belongs to Ann Trelonyan."

"Ann Trelonyan?"

"Yes, your old woman. You must see it before you go. I'll tell you how to find it. She bore the name of Trelonyan and was, according to Mary, a member of a distant branch of the family. It was a name quite widely borne at one time, but one never hears it now. In the few accounts her name is never given. They never say more than that one of the last-known witch killings in this part of Cornwall took place at Trelonyan Cove. But we have a lot more here. I'll read you parts of Mary's diary . . . not easy to read, but I've been through it carefully already and I've kept my eyesight."

Lyd sat opposite him in a low chair and waited in breathless interest to hear the diary of Mary Trelonyan.

Before he began to read Professor Tregowan handed the old leather-bound book to Lyd. On the fly leaf, in small, mannered writing, were the words: "The diary of Mary Trelonyan, started in this year of grace eighteen hundred and twelve."

"She only made a few entries a year until 1819," said the Professor, taking it back and turning the pages. "Poor woman, not much happened to her. An aging spinster daughter, living with her unpleasant old father and her brother and his wife. And not satisfied with her lot. Most of the early entries describe family quarrels and money troubles, but here and there a few words give a picture of how remote and cut off Trelonyan was. Here, in 1815:

"Sometimes it seems to me that I shall not survive sane for another year in this place, for I see few people apart from the immediate family circle. The fisherfolk who live around the Cove below are a rough lot. Most of them have never been more than a few miles from the village in their lives, and their lives are hard and narrow. They exist in poverty and misery and often in ill health, mainly subsisting on fish and the few vegetables they are able to grow in the poor soil by the sea.

They are inbred, ignorant, and subject to much ill fortune. Only last week, during a storm, three men were lost at sea."

Professor Tregowan paused and glanced at Lyd.

"You begin to get a picture, don't you? She was looking down on this from the high cliff. Never involved, though she would have liked to be."

"When I saw . . . last night . . . there were a lot of cottages," Lyd murmured. "Far more than now. Please go on."

"The children are wild and very ready to turn thieves. Yesterday Father caught two young boys stealing apples from our sheltered orchard. Needless to say, there are no apple trees down in the Cove. To my great horror, he beat them within an inch of their lives. The younger of the boys was the son of one of the men so recently drowned. No wonder my father is so much hated by these people. He has no feeling for their sad plight at all.

"If only Father would permit, I feel I might help and counsel these poor, ignorant folk. But he quite refuses to let me work among them, or even set foot in the Cove. The same rule applies to Sarah, my brother's wife, but Sarah doesn't mind. She has no taste, she says, for such charitable work. Sarah is content enough if she is able to drive occasionally into Penzance. She has her children, but I have nothing. I hate my father even more than the fisherfolk do. Yes, hate him. He is a hard, bad man and will do nothing for the people who are his tenants. He refuses to repair the cottages. There is little money in our family, I am aware of that. But the people in the Cove live like pigs and suffer. In consequence they are filled with fear and hate, and such emotions breed trouble."

Lyd shivered. She had seen some of the trouble that

ensued. She felt drawn back into that long-ago time when Trelonyan Manor was occupied and the Cove was peopled with struggling fisherfolk, with hate and fear in their hearts.

"This is 1816," said the Professor.

"Someone else, it seems, is helping the poor folk of the Cove. She came two years ago to live in a cottage up the lane, and her name is the same as ours. She is an Ann Trelonyan. She is old, and one of the maids told me that she came from Marazion, but I have no idea if that is true, or why she chose to live here. It is not a cottage that Father owns, or I feel sure he would not permit her to reside there. He says she must be a member of another branch of the family, with the members of which he had hard words nearly fifty years ago. But with whom has my father not had trouble? He cannot get on with anyone.

"This Ann Trelonyan is said to be a grandmother and a widow. Her son travels the world in a sailing ship, and no one knows where his wife and children are. She lives quietly with her cat and grows vegetables and herbs. Eliza, the maid, says she looks after the fisherfolk when they are ill, and is nigh to being a saint. I could wish I were regarded as a saint, but that is impossible. I do nothing, only live out my pointless days in this house, wishing for work to do. But my father, that great tyrant, watches me all the time."

"She *was* good . . . Ann Trelonyan," Lyd said. "I knew that all the time. So why . . . ?"

"Wait!" The Professor turned the pages. "We come to 1819.

"Today, May 20, is my birthday. Was ever anything more depressing? I am forty-five years old, unmarried, and with no prospect now of ever finding a husband. Whom have I ever been able to meet who would be suitable? We entertain not at all, and we are increasingly short of money. It is a beautiful day, hot, with a dark-blue sky. I stood on the cliff and looked down at the Cove. Lately there has been trouble there. The news came to me through Eliza, as usual. A child, doctored by Ann Trelonyan, died. No doubt she would have died in any case. Those poor folk are subject to so many ills. But the word is going around that Ann Trelonyan is not as clever or as good as people supposed. Eliza, who is an intelligent girl for her class, says she believes that a certain Adam Polpern is responsible for this. He has influence, and he hates Ann Trelonyan because she chided him for his cruel treatment of his wife.

"The people are easily swayed, and feeling is starting to run high. They say she is a witch and intended the child to die for some secret reason of her own. They are remembering that, last year, another unfortunate child died. They are so ignorant, so superstitious. I would not be Ann Trelonyan, living alone in that isolated cottage."

"Oh, how awful!" Lyd had seen that cottage.
The Professor nodded and went on.

"Then, in June . . . There was a summer storm, so violent that we feared the roof would be lifted off this house. During the storm a boat was lost with all hands. A hazard of nature, one would have said, but this morning Eliza came to me much upset by what she had heard. She has relatives down in the Cove. They are saying that Ann Trelonyan put the evil eye on the boat. They say she was there, and said something, made some sign, as the boats left the quay. Fear is indeed rampant down there in that place. Sorrow one could understand, but belief in witchcraft in this supposedly enlightened day and age . . . it is incredible. I was so much disturbed that I dared to go to Father and beg him, in all charity, to bring Ann Trelonyan here, but he was much annoyed with me. He was, indeed, at his worst. He is a wicked man, and his wickedness is worse than the fears of superstitious folk."

It was really becoming a story, part of history, rather than something Lyd herself had seen. It was terrible, but fascinating. She waited silently as the old man turned the pages.

"July," he said.

"Today I learned that feelings still run high down there in the Cove. Ann Trelonyan's cat was on the quay and one of the fishermen attempted to drown it, but the beast escaped. They do truly believe now that the cat is Ann Trelonyan in witch form. If I were Ann Trelonyan, I would go away, but it is possible she has nowhere to go.

"Eliza says also that there are a few families who are not in agreement with these beliefs. She mentioned particularly the Treporths, who are considerably more respectable than most of the fisherfolk. The father, Saul Treporth, has tried to persuade everyone that this whole story is a fabrication, but his youngest son, a wild lad and eager for trouble, has been in the forefront of the tormenting of Ann Trelonyan."

So Saul was right, Lyd said to herself. He'll be glad to know his family were better than most of them.

"And now August, 1819," said the Professor. "The very date, Lyd, so perhaps that's why you saw these things.

"Tonight there was a full moon. I could not sleep, so eventually I dressed again and let myself quietly out of the house. I walked to the cliff edge and looked down on the Cove. It was some time after midnight. Shouts had drawn me there, though I was much feared by what I should see. I now feel I shall never forget the horror of what I viewed. For they threw Ann Trelonyan into the water at high tide and, I think, threw her cat after her. I could see them all quite clearly in the brillance of the moonlight: their dark figures out there on the quay and the old woman struggling in deep water. Today I feel shame and bitterness, for I knew what was coming. At least I knew that they were ignorant folk, and I had read about the fate of women believed to be witches. But who would have thought, in this modern age, that such ignorance and super-stition could still bring death to an innocent woman in Trelonyan Cove?

"There are a few other entries," explained the Pro-fessor, looking at Lyd's absorbed face. "But mainly to do with her increasing hatred of her father and her desire to go away. She never did, poor woman. She lived a long time before Women's Lib. She lies buried in the church-yard here, only a few yards from Ann Trelonyan. But there is one last entry that applies. It was made about two weeks after the murder in the Cove.

"The terrible affair was hushed up and word given out that Ann Trelonyan slipped and drowned before she could be rescued. Ann Trelonyan lies in St. Buryan churchyard, and one can only hope she is now at peace. There were those, Eliza says, who argued that she should not be buried in consecrated ground. Many people still believe that she was a witch and received just punishment. Just! That poor, innocent soul! I never wish again to look down on the Cove."

"And after that," said the Professor, "the diary tails off into just an occasional entry. You've heard all that is important."

CHAPTER THIRTEEN

Mr. Allbright Opens a Box

"Mary Trelonyan should have helped!" Lyd cried fiercely. "She should have gone down to the Cove and talked to them, in spite of her father."

"She knew that herself," the Professor answered. "I'm sure she felt guilty for the rest of her life."

Lyd nodded, her mind more on Mary Trelonyan than on the scene she had witnessed in gauzy near-reality the previous night.

"You can't really blame Mary," the old man went on. "Women hadn't a hope in those days, not unless they were rich and powerful in their own right. The world still has many faults, but you're lucky. You can go out and say what you like—try to change things."

"Demonstrating and all that," mused Lyd.

He gave a wry smile. "I suppose so. I don't really approve of some of the capers young people get up to, but I'm too old to understand. It's better than living out an arid life, always frustrated and guilty."

The housekeeper knocked on the door and looked into the room. "There's a car waiting outside, sir," she said.

"I must go!" Lyd scrambled up out of the chair and

impulsively took the old man's had. "Thank you for reading the diary to me. It *has* made a difference to know more. There's one other thing I'd like to know. There are no fishermen living in Trelonyan Cove now, and I don't think there can have been for a long time. Was it because of what happened that they all went away?"

"I don't think it had much bearing on the murder of Ann Trelonyan," he said slowly. "It was more likely tied up with the fading fortunes of the Trelonyans at the Manor. The cottages they owned would gradually get into such a bad state that people had to go. And fishing has had its very bad times. Trelonyan Cove isn't the only place that has no fishing boats now. I do know that by 1870, when the Manor was empty, there were only a few families left. But they stayed for some years. I used to know an old man who was a boy there in the eighteen nineties, and his sons and their families lived there until the Second World War. After the war the remaining cottages belonged to retired people. Now they're mostly empty, I gather."

"It's rather sad," said Lyd. "Where is Ann Trelonyan's grave, please?"

He told her the exact spot, and Lyd went to join her family. They all went together to the churchyard, which was dominated by the great tower of the church. As they went, Lyd told them something of what she had heard. They found the grave without much difficulty. It was deep in grass and brambles in a far corner, but though the words were faint and in old lettering, they were just discernible.

Here lies the body of Ann Trelonyan
drowned in Trelonyan Cove, August 25, 1819
She rests in peace

They set off to drive through the long miles of Cornwall, with Lyd in the back of the car, as she had come. Only now, strangely, she didn't feel so desperately uncomfortable or shut in. She sat relaxed, occasionally slipping against Tom's shoulder as they went around a curve.

She was quiet; they were all rather quiet. She still felt guilty over the trouble and worry she had caused, but the boys didn't seem to hold it against her. When they did speak it was about things at home in Bristol and about the coming prospects of various football teams. Lyd didn't really greatly care about professional football, but the boys had seen that she had some knowledge. She was glad that there was no feeling of strain between her and her brothers.

Tom and Jeff were still puzzled over what had happened, but they had agreed, privately, that they wouldn't ask any more questions. All that business of Lyd listening to an old diary and seeking out an old grave in St. Buryan churchyard seemed peculiar, but once home, she would be all right. She seemed all right now, not even minding the narrow confines of the car and Collie sitting on her feet.

Lyd did feel, in a strange way, almost at peace. She had parted in a friendly way from Saul, and she was convinced that she really would see him again. Part of her silence was that she was thinking about him, remembering so many things with warm pleasure. She had learned a lot from knowing Saul, and it *couldn't* be that they would never meet again. She wondered, too, why she didn't mind the car anymore. Could one really lose a deep-seated fear so quickly? Maybe it was because she had faced so many other things and grown up.

She was just a trifle worried, because her parents, in the front seat, were so silent. Yet she was sure they were not annoyed with her. Her mother merely looked troubled, or perhaps puzzled, and her father seemed to be thinking deeply, unless he was simply concentrating on the road ahead.

Possibly he didn't believe her even now; Lyd didn't blame him at all if that was the case. As they drove over the bridge across the River Tamar, the whole affair began to seem like a dream.

That was the last of Cornwall, and she felt sad for a time. Cornwall was Saul's county, and possibly her own. Even now, Saul was there in the Cove, working hard, as he would be until late September. Then he would work for a year, both at the Penzance job and at his books.

The car was going fairly well with the new battery, but it was still old, and traffic was heavy. They had stopped for a time to eat their picnic lunch, and now it was nearly five o'clock, so when Mr. Allbright saw a bed-and-break-fast sign near Exeter, he turned the car off the road. The woman in charge said she could put them up, if they would share two rooms. One room held two big beds, ample space for Mr. Allbright and the boys.

Lyd was glad to sleep with her mother. They went to bed early and she was soon in deep unconsciousness. But Mrs. Allbright lay awake for a while, because she could not forget a short private conversation she had had with her husband as they took a walk after supper.

"What's the matter?" she had asked. "It's all over, isn't it? Except for Lyd and Saul. I think we'll have to ask him to stay with us before the summer is really over. We can put up the camp bed in the living room."

"You mean you're encouraging our daughter to have a boy friend?"

"Not a boy friend merely. A friend. He's a nice lad, and she had to find someone soon. I'd sooner it were Saul than some of the boys there are around. He won't be silly or too precipitate. He has his way to make, and so has Lyd. She's very young yet. But they can meet sometimes, and be good friends. So what's worrying you?"

"I've remembered something, that's all," Mr. Allbright had answered. "It's been nagging at my mind for days. I can't be sure until I can check."

"To do with Lyd?"

"Yes. I may be wildly out, but I think. . . . Wait until we reach home."

They arrived in Bristol at twelve o'clock the next day. Lyd found it very strange, and rather pleasant, to be back in her own room among her books and other possessions. She busied herself with unpacking and helping her mother. They had lunch around one-thirty; then Tom and Jeff went off to find some of their friends, and Lyd went to the library to borrow something new to read.

While she was away Mr. Allbright brought out a small steel box and unlocked it, with his wife watching curiously.

"What's in there?" she asked. "Oh, your insurance policies and our marriage certificate and the boys' birth certificates. I know that. Something else?"

"Lyd's papers," said Mr. Allbright.

His wife came to stand beside him. She had forgotten that Lyd had papers other than the adoption certificate, and she hadn't seen that since the adoption went through so many years ago.

At the bottom of the box, under all the other things, was a large brown envelope. Mr. Allbright opened it and took out some loose papers and some smaller envelopes and spread them on the table.

"It wasn't quite a usual adoption," he said. "I mean

she wasn't a baby, or illegitimate, or anything like that. The Matron at the Home gave me all these in case I ever felt it wise to pass them on to Lyd when she was older. Yes, I thought so! I knew I'd seen the name somewhere, or heard it. I said so, when first I learned about the cottage at Trelonyan Cove."

"But—"

"Look!" His fair, ordinary face was troubled and more puzzled than it had been during the strange holiday. "Lyd's mother was an Ann Trelonyan. She lived in Liskeard, Cornwall, and married a Robert Pratt in Bodmin. Here are letters—I never read them—written by Robert Pratt to Ann Trelonyan before they were married. There are some photographs in this envelope." He glanced at them briefly, turning to the back of each. "Ann Trelonyan as a schoolgirl. Lyd is very much like her. And Lyd as a baby. Look at this one of Lyd with both parents. At two, Lyd was just her mother over again, and *she* was Cornish."

"So was that why . . . ?" Mrs. Allbright leaned heavily against the table. "Lyd belonged. I know Liskeard is in East Cornwall—we came through it not long before crossing back over the bridge—and far from Trelonyan Cove. But was that old woman of hers an ancestor?"

"It looks like it. I suppose we shall never know for certain. It may have been so. If Lyd is interested enough she can maybe trace it back one day. There must be parish records. The whole thing is really beyond me."

"Are you going to tell Lyd now, show her these papers?"

"I don't know what to do," he said doubtfully. "She's our girl. I don't want to do anything that will make her feel she doesn't belong to us. Maybe it's better not."

"She isn't really a child anymore. Soon she'll be a woman. She may want to know. It explains so much, in a way."

"It explains nothing to me," said her husband. "I'm a

practical man. There seems to be no doubt that Lyd experienced something in the Cove, but I shall never really understand it and I'd prefer it be forgotten. Lyd is ours. She belongs to us just as much as if she were our own girl."

"I know. I don't want anything to come between us, but I don't think it will. The last few days we've been able to talk to Lyd more easily than for years. I've felt closer, as if a barrier had been removed. I think you must tell her."

Lyd surprised them by returning home then. She had found books quickly and hurried back, for she had a strange feeling that she wanted to be with her parents.

"What's up?" she asked, seeing their guilty starts and the papers spread out on the table.

Mrs. Allbright then made a decision, sure that it was the right one. "Lyd, we have something to tell you . . . show you. It's here in these old papers. It's a very strange thing, dear, but it does seem to be some kind of explanation."

Her father glanced at Lyd and suddenly decided that she could take it, and that *they* would have to stand by her reaction. He hated anything that made Lyd remember she had other beginnings, but it did seem right.

"Lyd," he said, "there's a good deal we've never talked about. I didn't want to. It never seemed necessary. Maybe it was wrong. In the first place you didn't know that your parents died in a car crash."

Lyd stood very still, staring at them.

"How?" Suddenly all the fears that she had ever felt in the family car rushed in on her.

"Some crazy driver on a bend. Your parents' car was driven up a bank and burst into flames. You were with them, but you were thrown clear. They died almost instantly."

"So was that why . . . why I was always scared? I didn't

remember, not with my conscious mind. But I hated to be trapped." Amazingly, she could speak of it now.

"I suppose so," he said reluctantly. "We hoped you'd get over it."

"Do you know?" said Lyd, easy with wonderful knowledge. "I think I have. Maybe not entirely, but coming home I felt much better. I was always so ashamed, for there seemed to be no reason—"

"There was reason. Well, they left hardly any money, just enough, when everything was sold, for funeral expenses and to keep you for a few weeks. For a short time you were taken by the woman next door, while their furniture and possessions were sold or disposed of. That kind woman kept some papers, and they were sent to the Home with you: your parents' marriage certificate, a copy of your birth certificate, photographs, and some letters written by your father to your mother before they were married."

"Yes, Dad." Lyd walked slowly toward the table.

"It's no real explanation to me, but you may feel differently. I had forgotten, but coming back from Cornwall, I half remembered. Before her marriage to Robert Pratt your mother's name was Ann Trelonyan."

Lyd took it quietly, as if she had always known.

"Was that why it all happened to me? I *was* connected in some way. That old woman was my great-great-grandmother? Or would it be a few more greats?"

They looked at her, across the papers spread out on the table.

"You'd better look at them all," her father said. "There's a picture of you with your real parents when you were only two. It must have been taken just before the accident."

Lyd took the photographs first, and stared at them.

Her mother was dark-haired and had a happy expression. Then she picked up the letters; there were only five of them, still in their envelopes with post marks. They might, she thought dazedly, tell her something about Ann Trelonyan . . . the original Ann Trelonyan. But when she glanced at the letters, they told her nothing, even about her real father. Robert Pratt had been no very able correspondent. The letters fixed dates for future meetings, made plans for the wedding. There were few words of love, and they created no image of a real person.

She put down the last of the letters slowly and glanced at the two people who had been her father and mother for as long as she could remember. In a moment of sharp awareness, she knew that what she said now was important, far more important than the strange fact of her mother bearing the name of Ann Trelonyan.

She saw the shadows under her adoptive mother's eyes and felt the tension, the carefully hidden anxiety, and her heart was filled with such a rush of love and need that she could only think of them. *They* were her father and mother, these two people waiting in silence.

Lyd knew, too, in those moments of awareness, that she was not really like them. Without conceit, she knew that she was clever and might one day learn and understand things that were not part of their lives. She might go on into a different, wider world, as she would have gone from her real parents, had they lived. But not yet. Oh, not yet! Here she was, at home, with the only parents she had ever known.

"Lock all these things up again, please, Dad." she said steadily. "I'm glad I've seen them. It *was* because I belonged to that place, I suppose. My mother may have lived in Liskeard, but her roots went back to that old woman who died in Trelonyan Cove. I'm glad I under-

stand, but I want to be Lyd Allbright. Oh, Mother, I *am*
Lyd Allbright, aren't I?" And, forgetting all tensions
and barriers, forgetting that she was sixteen, she went into
her mother's arms.

"Of course, love. You belong to us. We only told you
because it was a kind of explanation. We won't speak of
it again." Over Lyd's small dark head Mr. and Mrs. Allbright exchanged glances of relief and joy.

"I'll tell Saul about my connection with Ann Trelonyan. I'll write to him now."

"Yes, do write him a letter," said her mother. "Tell him
he may come here any time that his uncle can bring him
up to Bristol. We'll be glad to see him."

Lyd went slowly to her room. Trelonyan Cove, she
thought. Somehow a line of people went back to that old
woman who had been drowned by ignorant, superstitious
people. She was said to have been a grandmother, so
there must have been children somewhere who grew up
and married. Maybe they never even knew what had
happened to the solitary old woman and her cat and were
ignorant of the loneliness and the terror and the way it all
ended on that night of brilliant moonlight. It had been
left to her, Lyd Allbright, to see it and know it. Fate,
chance, or some obscure design had taken her to Trelonyan Cove in an August far distant from those days,
and, in ghostly fashion, the thing had been played out.

Could she ever go back to Trelonyan Cove? If Saul
were to stay in her life she might have to. But she had the
strange conviction that her ghostly experience would not
happen again, that the shadows and the old fears had
faded at last, had been worked out, worn out, because a
modern girl, with some of the same blood in her veins,
had been there at the right time and had witnessed the
old tragedy.

"She rests in peace." Probably she did, in that Cornish earth that was not so very many miles away from Trelonyan Cove. And it was to be hoped that Mary Trelonyan lay in peace also. Lyd was suddenly, violently glad that she lived in another age, when she could make her own destiny and fight against things that she thought wrong. Her parents would not hold her, whatever she planned to do.

She was Lyd Allbright, and that was important. Not Lyd Pratt. She had made her choice, and now she could talk to the people nearest to her.

But Saul had to know about the thread that bound her to Trelonyan Cove, and maybe, some day, Professor Tregowan must know, too. He would be interested. Lyd found writing paper and an envelope and began a long letter to Saul.